Disappearing Act

Ray Pace

Copyright © 2021 Ray Pace

All rights reserved.

ISBN: **9798703467077**

For Julia

A special shout-out goes to writers who have persevered despite the Pandemic and raging storms of fire, rain, and ignorance. Somehow, we've managed to keep on doing what we do, minus the luncheon meetings and book parties. We've even managed to meet each other's pets via Zoom meetings.

"Disbelief in magic can force a poor soul into believing in government and business."

Tom Robbins

"The greatest escape I ever made was when I left Appleton, Wisconsin."

Harry Houdini

Chapter One

"Let me get this straight," I said. "You want me to go to Las Vegas to find some guy who owes us money."

Jacky nodded, put his fingertips together, and managed to look like a Buddha. If a Buddha were to wear a Chicago Bears sweatshirt and sit sipping Jack Daniels on the nineteenth-floor balcony of 1040 Lakeshore Drive.

"This guy is in Vegas?"

"As far as we know."

"How much does he owe?"

"Two million."

"Gambler?"

"Magician. He disappeared suddenly. He was renting the theater at Galloping Dominos."

"So, you want me to go to Vegas and un-disappear some magician that owes us two huge? In other words, put the rabbit back into the hat?" I looked at my watch. "The date on my Rolex doesn't say April first, Jacky."

Jacky smiled, reached over the wrought iron table, and poured more whiskey into our glasses.

"I know you can do it, Nick. We've booked you on the redeye out of O'Hare tonight. Take you two, three days. There are some old friends out there. They can help."

"You sweet talking me, Jacky?"

He did the Buddha finger-tips thing again and smiled.

"Someday, Jacky, I'm gonna come into about six million bucks..."

"Yeah, I know that old saw, Nick. You'll never walk away. You'd put the six mil on red and give the wheel a turn. You'd die without the action."

It was no use arguing with him. He knew me. Give me a challenge, something to figure out, and I was like the dog with a new rawhide bone,

I gave him my charming grin, picked up my Delta tickets, and smiled some more.

"I'll go out there and take a look around."

"You'll do fine, Nick. You'll do fine."

I thought about how I was going to handle our disappearing magician as the plane made its way to Vegas. It's true that people go to Sin City and disappear. Sometimes they disappear one identity in favor of a new one. Divorce, remarriage is part of it. Then there's the method of where someone disappears someone else, usually over money or another kind of betrayal. The desert is full of ghosts. Skeletons show up from time to time.

Usually, there's a line on people if you look hard and know who to talk to.

The word was that this magician, Charlemagne, had one of the hottest shows in Vegas. The house was packed every night. Two months ago, he quit paying his rent. A few days back, he disappeared. The whole show vanished. No trace.

Or so they said.

My first stop was the Galloping Dominos Casino and a heart to heart with Neal Braxton, who supposedly ran the theater. I knew him from Chicago. We didn't hang out together, but we traveled in the same circle. *Capisce?*

Braxton always seemed a little too loose for my taste. I couldn't make up my mind if he was a coked-up hipster, or just some ass kisser who couldn't be trusted. He was always a little too agreeable with the people he was talking with at the time.

"Nick, good to see you," he said as I entered his office. "How are Jacky and the rest of my friends in Chicago?"

"They're a little forlorn," I said. "They're missing their friend Charlemagne and the treasure chest he took with him. With your cooperation, I'll head for his forwarding address and square things up with our magical friend."

"Hah," he said. "Wish I could help you there."

He tossed his hands up in the air like he was about to signal two-thirds of a touchdown.

"Yeah, I wish you could help, too," I said. "Because if you can't, Jacky's going to be pissed, and you don't want that. I don't want that either."

"You're right," he said. "But there isn't a line on any of those people in Charlemagne's show. They just vanished. It's like they were ghosts."

"What do you mean? Ghosts?"

"This ain't that big a town," Braxton said, leaning forward on his desk like he was about to take an order at a pizza joint. "Everybody knows somebody, but no one knows anybody in Charlemagne's show. Nobody was screwing any of the women. Nobody knew any of the technicians. Nobody could even swear to you what Charlemagne looked like out of his costume. Whoever they are, they kept to themselves."

"Are you telling me you never met Charlemagne?"

"I met his manager, Ted Evans, who forked over the million every month. I took him through the facilities when we made the deal, just like Jacky said to do. Take a million out front and let them have the keys to the theatre. Whatever this guy Charlemagne was going to do, would be a hell of a lot better than the Liberace impersonator that fell on his ass there. Jesus. That show was god awful. I told that to Jacky out in front. The young fags don't know who Liberace was, and the old ladies that liked the guy are all dead."

So much for enlightenment among casino operators. I tried to steer Braxton back to the business at hand.

"Ted Evans. That's the manager, right?"

"Yeah." Braxton lit a cigarette. "Big fat guy with an old desert rat beard. He wears those flowered cowboy shirts. Smells like he stepped in horseshit. A real character, but his cash was good. Jacky knows that. Probably still has most of it, unless he bet it on the Bears."

"So, where does this guy Evans stay? He must have a room somewhere. Where's he hang out? Shit, they have to eat. Have to sleep somewhere?

Braxton signaled for two-thirds of another touchdown.

I didn't want to lean on him too heavy. Maybe he was telling it like it was.

I took the keys to the vacant theatre from Braxton and told him I'd look around. In the meantime, I wanted him to get me some shots of Evans off the security cams. Maybe I could find someone who at least knew him by sight.

"Hell, all he'd have to do to disappear is shave his beard," Braxton said.

I looked at Braxton and wondered how someone like him ended up at the Galloping Dominos. Good taste, I decided, had nothing to do with it.

Braxton was typical of Vegas, an over-blown loser who fit perfectly into the culture of what some my Chicago people call Loser-Land.

"Nick," I can hear you say, "Shouldn't you be the kind of guys that love Las Vegas? You Chicago guys?" Wink, wink?

Yeah, Chicago guys. I should start a group called "Chicago Lives Matter" so we can all be defended from know-it-alls. We won't have to listen to some Eastern experts expound on how we all like our hotdogs without ketchup. We all want our pizzas with a thick crust. We all suffer from the Cubs and get our hearts broken each year by the Bears. And, oh yeah, we all know some fantastic place to go hear the blues. It's right next door to an Italian restaurant where everybody there is connected to the Mafia.

Stereotypes.

I smother my hotdogs in ketchup and anything else I can get my hands on. The fact is you could leave out the hotdog. I'd never miss it.

I like the thin-crusted pizza.

I expect the Cubs and the Bears to lose more than their share, and I bet accordingly. The blues are best at a lakefront festival, not in some Southside rat-hole. As far as the Italian restaurant where the Mafia hangs out, well, we don't use that disgusting ethnic slur. In Chicago, we refer to it as The Outfit.

Chicago used to love Vegas, but Vegas has taken a dive. The high rollers are in Macau. Vegas, according to some Chicago associates, is where shoe store managers go to play Sinatra. Ring-a-ding-ding, my ass.

Anyhow, a shoe store manager playing Sinatra wasn't on my current dance card. Finding Charlemagne and the two million he owed Jacky was.

I walked over to the theatre and let myself in with the keys Braxton gave me. It was clean as in "too clean." Whoever had done the cleanup when Charlemagne decided to boogie could have been from the CIA doing one of those Area 51 cleanups. The only DNA in the place I thought as I walked through was coming from me.

I spent a couple of hours looking through the place. I was about to leave empty-handed when I noticed an old over-stuffed chair next to the loading dock door. It might have been for a security guard taking in deliveries. I reached beside the cushion. Something was down in the crack. A small plastic bag with about a dozen coins inside: next to it was half a pack of *Gauloise* cigarettes.

Did I find a real clue, or was this just the stash of some underpaid working stiff who no longer worked in the theatre? How long had this stuff been sitting there? The chair was beat-up. Most people wouldn't sit in it.

I shoved the stuff into my pocket and locked the place up.

Back at Braxton's office, I picked up six stills of Ted Evans from the security cams at the Galloping Dominos. Evans looked pretty much what Braxton had described. Behind the beard, he could have been anybody.

CHAPTER TWO

I headed over to the Dominic's Sports Betting Parlor on the strip. I knew I'd find Jimmy Cox there. You could call it his office, but he wouldn't be the one answering the phone. He was one of their more exciting customers. He had moved to Vegas from Franklin Park, outside of Chicago.

He had been a lawyer in Illinois. He had carried the ball for Jacky for problems at Club Ali Bam in North Lake. Gambling and prostitution were frequent legal problems on the premises.

If North Lake sounds like a scenic town, guess again. It's named after an industrial intersection of North Avenue and Lake Street.

Jimmy didn't practice law anymore. His retirement came out of an agreement with the Illinois Bureau of Investigation and an influential politician from Chicago's Southside who told the IBI that all should be forgotten. Allegations of Jimmy Cox bribing a Republican Senator and a Democrat congressman were dropped. Retirement to Nevada by Lawyer Cox was a big part of the deal. Everybody involved wanted it all to go away.

Jimmy sat in his favorite spot. He could watch all the monitors from sporting events around the world. He could also watch many of the bettors, and to Jimmy, that was as important as an insider's report on Wall Street.

"Watch what Dinkins does on that sixth race at Gulfstream," he said as I approached where he sat. "He's been sitting there all afternoon doing nothing. He's getting ready to plunge."

I nodded.

Jimmy nodded and watched Dinkins.

Dinkins nodded at Jimmy.

Jimmy raised his hand and spread his fingers.

"Five," he said.

Dinkins nodded.

We were good at nodding.

"How's Jacky," Jimmy said. It wasn't a question.

"Fine," I said. It wasn't an answer.

"Good," Jimmy said. "You must be here trying to find Aladdin or Houdini or whatever his name is. I hear he's into Jacky big time."

I nodded.

"That guy Braxton let that magician slide out without paying," Jimmy said. "That Neal's a real jerk. Christ's sake, is that the best we can do these days?"

I nodded again.

"Find anything to go on?"

I showed him the photos of Ted Evans.

He nodded.

"This guy for real?"

"Hell," I said. "As far as I know, none of this is for real."

I showed him the pack of cigarettes and the plastic bag of coins.

"Not much to go on," He said. "This belongs to some cheap French hooker?"

I laughed.

He nodded, then said, "You know, almost nobody uses quarters anymore. It's all electronic. Most of the slot machines don't take coins. Hell, not even the Laundromats. You buy a card with so much on it and use it on the washers and dryers. It makes it harder to launder money through self-serve laundries."

I told him where I was staying. I'd think about what he said, and I'd get back to him. I headed to the hotel to check in.

There was a message on my phone in the hotel suite. Could I call Cassandra Black at the Las Vegas Star Review? She heard from Jimmy Cox that I was in town. She might have some information about Charlemagne that I'd be interested in hearing.

I was about to return her call when there was a knock on the door.

Two suits wearing dark sunglasses stood in the hall. The thinner of the two spoke while the fat one nodded and grunted.

"We heard you were in town," the thin guy said. "We're from the FBI Special Projects Criminal Terrorist Section."

They both flashed IDs.

I was surprised that they didn't have dark glasses on in their ID photos.

I invited them in. Agents Fitch and Rice.

"There's a possible connection between Charlemagne and a foreign group," Rice said.

"Yeah," I said. "Cirque du Soleil."

Rice began scanning the room with his eyes. Maybe he thought I was hiding Charlemagne in the bathroom or under the bed.

"No, we're serious," Fitch said.

"So, you guys are looking for him, too?" I asked. "I'm only interested in collecting some money he owes us. You think he's some kind of terrorist?"

"Didn't say that," Rice said. "Let's just say we're interested in any help you can give us."

"Likewise, I'm sure," I said. "You guys got any kind of a lead on him you'd care to share?"

"Not right now," Rice said. "Here's my card. Call me any time, day or night. One other thing, this Charlemagne character is dangerous. Don't think you can handle him by yourself."

"How'd you guys get wind of my being in town, or is that a state secret?" I asked.

"You show up in our database from time to time," Rice said. "Let's just say you're one of our more interesting persons of interest."

Fitch stared at Rice and made a "let's go" flip with his head.

They left. Their business card had heavy raised type on it. I wondered if it had micro circuitry under the ink – a perfect way to track someone. I wrote the info from the card into my notebook and headed out.

I could have walked to Cassandra Black's office, but my ulterior motive had me grabbing a taxi. As I exited the cab in front of the Las Vegas Star Review, I dropped the FBI business card behind the rear seat cushion. From the looks of the cab's littered interior, the card would be riding around town for the next few weeks. Agents Fitch and Rice might be following.

Cassandra ushered me into her private office. She was a beautiful woman in her late thirties and looked like she'd stay that way forever. Cassandra knew how to use her good looks and her brains to build her news and entertainment website up from nothing.

"She decided she wanted to be dealt into the game," Jacky had said. "When the major players didn't move fast enough to let her in, she jumped the line."

She got a major developer to back her. In turn, she threw all her support in back of their project. She managed to sell it to the powers-that-be, even though it was way too big and verging on the obnoxious. It was all planned. The developers didn't want to go that big. Actually, they couldn't afford it.

At that point, she formed a civic group that wanted to scale back the project. Her website got behind that. The developer agreed. The city government got off the hook on sewer bills that would have run into millions—sharp lady, all around.

I sat in the sharp lady's office, looking at a bunch of awards on display.

"Nick," she looked at me from across her mahogany desk. "How's Jacky? When's he coming out?"

"Jacky's fine, except he's a little light in the pocket due to our friend Charlemagne," I said. "I'm out here trying to do the impossible trick of un-disappearing a magician. Maybe I should go over and see Penn and Teller. See what kind of ideas they have on the subject."

She smiled.

I gave her my crooked grin.

"It ain't magic, Nick," she said. "It never was. I caught the Charlemagne act several times. This was something else. Being in that theatre was like being in some sort of a fourth or fifth dimension. People walked out of there stunned. It was enough to make you start believing in the Devil or witchcraft. I've seen a lot of shows on the strip. This was nothing like the others. All the others you can figure out. All the magicians on the strip tried to figure it out. They never got past first base."

Cassandra could read people and get them to open up. I asked her if she had ever met Ted Evans, Charlemagne's manager. Neal Braxton had described him as fat horseshit wearing a beard and cowboy shirt. His photos off the security cams didn't dispute Braxton's point.

"My God, yes," she leaned forward. "He's an interesting character. Several times I interviewed him. He'd refer to himself as Old Zeke."

"Old Zeke?" I asked. "Like an old cowhand?"

"Maybe," she said. "He had a lot to say about the old days when people had more respect for others, and religion really meant survival. He said he had hopes that Charlemagne's show would break people out of their troubled lives. Evans is one of those people who respect the desert. He'd talk about it mystically. About righteousness coming out of an approaching storm and floods washing things away. If you've ever seen a flash flood out here, it's impressive. People drown in the desert. Imagine that. It was one Hell of a show. You never saw it, Nick?"

I shook my head.

"It was out to break all conventions," she said. "Not just the nudity and the shooting money into the audience. There was this whole thing about spatial relationships. Things got bigger and smaller and changed colors and disappeared. It was like a challenge to reality. While you were in that show, it was as if you gave up every notion of what was real and what was fantasy."

"I had a visit from the feds before I came over," I said. "They wanted to know what I knew about our boy Charlemagne. FBI Special Projects Criminal Terrorist Section."

"Two suits named Fitch and Rice," she said. "They've been all over the strip looking for a lead on Charlemagne. I don't think they're who they claim to be."

I was interested.

"Who do you think they are?"

"Not who they say they are," she said. "One of my contacts works over at the city jail. Roland. Nice guy. Gives us the old heads up when he gets an interesting boarder at his hotel. Working gal got busted trying to steal a couple of wallets from two johns she was partying with. Your pals, Rice and Fitch. In the end, all they wanted was all their wallets and toys back. Drop the charges, they said, but that's not what Doris, the working gal said about it. She claims these two got high on coke. They started talking about working at Area 51 and some sort of space warping project."

CHAPTER THREE

Cassandra couldn't tell me anything more. I decided to walk back to my hotel and take in some of the sights along the strip.

I picked up two unforgettable sights when I stopped in front of Bellagio to watch the fountain show. Two mugs a hundred feet down from me had walked behind me from Cassandra's office.

They looked like they had strolled out of a cut-rate commercial for resort wear. They were wearing white fedoras with black hatbands, seersucker jackets, and white shoes. They both weighed over 300 pounds. They had poured themselves into what a guy weighing 250 would fit into just right. It made them stand out like a Salvation Army lassie in a whorehouse.

If this was trouble, it came in the Vegas version of a clown suit.

They followed me into the casino. I turned past the blackjack tables and made a left into the arcade section where some of the nicer shops were open. Vegas being Vegas, my guess was the shops were always open.

I went into the gelato shop and ordered blueberry topped with a scoop of espresso deluxe. From the corner, I could watch my two friends enter the shop. I could hear them order from the counter guy. Both had Russian accents. If these guys were really on my tail, I was now involved in international intrigue.

I had to make sure.

I hated the thought of leaving delicious gelato, but I stood up and headed for the door. Would my two Russian Bloodhounds follow?

"Make orders to go," I heard one of the men bellow to the guy behind the counter. "Hurry, I give big tip."

I walked back toward the blackjack tables, giving my new friends a chance to catch up if they were interested in me. They were. They followed at a distance, trying not to look like they were - which made it doubly comical.

I walked them around the Bellagio for half an hour. Speeding up, slowing down, and making false moves, had them stumbling. Finally, in the colorfully decorated atrium, I turned and walked up to them face-to-face.

"You two birds looking for me, or looking for trouble in general?" I asked.

"No, no, big mistake," the fatter of the two said.

"Yeah, big mistake, you guys got caught," I said. "I'm real tight with the management here, boys. I've waltzed you past every security cam in the joint. I can get an FBI make on you in seconds if you like."

The fatter guy couldn't come up with an answer, but his

partner was quicker.

"No, no, just talk," he stammered. "Just want talk, no trouble. Buy you drink in lounge. Just talk."

I stared at him for a minute.

"Hold on," I said.

I walked toward the check-in desk and waved at the guy behind the counter.

"Hey, Eddie," I said. "Tell Vince I'm talking with these two gents in the lounge."

The counter guy waved back like he knew me. I wondered if his name was really Eddie.

"Let's go, Slim," I said to the thinner of the two men.

We sat in three cushioned barstools at one of those waist-high tables. The waitress was quick on the draw, and before we knew it, we were sucking on three scotch and sodas.

"You are detective, private, yes," Slim said. It could have been either a question or an accusation in a Moscow courtroom.

"You could say that," I said. "You boys need some help with heavy lifting?"

The fatter guy spoke up.

"We try to find magician. Want to offer him big deal in Russia. Moscow. Big show. Big contract. Many big bucks, like you say here."

"I take it you've seen his show. What makes you think I can find him?"

"We follow you from Galloping Dominos," Slim said. "Neal Braxton owes us favor. He says you collect for Jacky in Chicago. You find Charlemagne. We pay you, too. Have offer he take big time, yeah."

I shot them a ridiculously high figure for delivering Charlemagne - $100,000.

"Yah, yah," Slim said way too fast. "We could make that work."

"Give me some info on how to find you guys," I said. "Cell phone, hotel?"

The fatter guy, Boris, handed me a business card from a whorehouse in Pahrump, Nevada. His cell phone number was written on the back.

Alexi, the thinner of the two fat men, shook my hand with an elaborate flourish. I thought I had just won the Olympic decathlon. Boris followed him out after giving me a semi- bear hug and saying, "Big money. Find magician. All cash dollars."

CHAPTER FOUR

After waltzing the two Russian bears around in the Bellagio, I decided to take an evening drive in the rental. Yogi Berra once said, "You can't hit and think at the same time." For me, I think better when I drive. Inside a car is one of the last places left where there's privacy.

I kept my eye on the rearview mirrors. I wondered if any of the cars behind me held the two Russians or agents Fitch and Rice from whatever planet or dimension they originated.

I turned onto Tropicana Avenue. I thought about the sack of coins and the half pack of French cigarettes I had found at the theater at Galloping Dominos. Whoever put the coins there was a smoker. And French cigarettes were a way to stand out. A show-off, I thought.

Watch me smoke foreign cigarettes at the laundromat? That didn't seem right. Besides, laundry machines now took electronic cash cards. Money was in digits. No more quarters there.

I glanced over to my left and saw it, The Pinball Hall of Fame. The sign outside said over a hundred pinball machines were in the place, and they were playable for a quarter.

It was a crazy notion. I'd stroll into the place and find Ted Evans with his full beard playing Pinball Wizard while smoking a *Gauloise*. In ten minutes, I'd have a line on Charlemagne and be on the road to collecting the two million bucks owed to Jacky.

I walked in. The place was humming with people playing pinball. Off to one side was a large change machine with a sign that said, "Five Dollars for 20 Quarters/ 20 Plays." I walked the aisles of pinball machines. It was an amazing collection. Pinball machines from the forties stood next to pinball machines designed around Star Trek and Star Wars.

I looked down all the aisles and found no one resembling the bearded Ted Evans, if that was really his name, and if that was really his beard. A thin guy behind the counter stood talking with a bleached-out blonde holding a purple poodle in her arms. The dog was anxious to go, shaking itself and trying to gain traction in mid-air while the blonde held it tight.

"I have to take Zuzu out to tinkle," Blondie said.

"Yeah, I don't want to mop the place again," the counter guy said.

Zuzu and Blondie left to go water the asphalt outside.

I walked up to the counter and showed the counter guy a photo of Evans.

"Ever see this guy hangin' out here?" I asked.

"Who are you? What'd he do?" The guy wanted answers.

"Call me Nick. I'm investigating the disappearance of Charlemagne from the Galloping Dominos. This guy's supposedly his manager."

"Yeah, I heard about that." He looked at the photo of Evans and coughed as if he had been smoking the *Gauloise* cigarettes.

"No, can't help you there," he said. "What makes you think he might be here?"

I tossed the plastic bag of coins onto the counter.

"This is one of the clues," I said. "It seems like you're one of the few places left that uses lots of quarters. We found these in the back of the theater at Galloping Dominos. Maybe this guy hangs out here and had some quarters left. Maybe he'd come back to play here."

"Yeah, makes sense," the guy said, looking at the sack of coins. "The only thing is, these coins won't work here."

I looked at him, thinking I must have read the sign on the change machine wrong. A five-dollar bill would get you a five-dollar electronic card, instead of quarters?

"Yeah, these aren't quarters," he said. "They're for that batting cage place south of the airport. See it says so right on the coin. Easy to mistake if you don't look close."

He was right. The coins were for a different sort of fantasy trip. Why settle for Pinball Wizard when you could be Home Run Hero?

I should have paid more attention. The coins weren't quarters.

I should have paid even more attention to the thug that followed me out to the parking lot where Purple Poodle was pissing a lake against one of the tires on the rental car.

The thug came up on my left side and shoved me against the hood of a Mercedes.

"I saw what you were showing that guy inside," he said. "Gimme it, right now, and no one gets hurt."

He was big in a worn-out athletic way –football hero at Southern Cracker College who majored in drinking and ended up getting a doctorate in drunk.

I reached in my jacket pocket as he held me to the car hood.

"Give me a chance to get it out, for Christ's sake," I said. "What the hell you want a bag of coins for?"

"You have it," he said. "We want it."

"You'll get it," I said.

I came out of my pocket with my brass knuckles and walloped him on the left temple. He staggered back. Bleached-out Blonde screamed when she saw the fight. Purple Poodle snarled and tried to bite her.

Southern Cracker Hero came back for more.

I swung again, and this time he blocked my swing with his wrist. I could hear something crack as I hit.

He backed away, holding his arm and ran toward Tropicana Avenue.

I chased.

We ran past the parked cars in the lot. I tried to lunge for him as we made the sidewalk, but he jumped aside and ran into the street.

Big mistake.

There was no way the tour bus could stop. First, he got slammed, and then he got squished. Bleached-out Blonde screamed again. This time Purple Poodle did bite her.

I jumped into the rental and drove out of the lot. I headed south on the strip toward the Vegas version of "Field of Dreams."

CHAPTER FIVE

I drove south on the strip past an evening of visitors who were out sampling Sin City and doing their own versions of "What you do in Vegas stays in Vegas." For most, it meant a couple of bad hangovers, losing a few hundred bucks, and seeing some shows. The shows ranged from the high-priced Celine Dion down to the pathetic lounge acts by hangers-on who had no place to go after Vegas. An overpriced drink got you front-row seating. If you wanted Celine or Cher, you were talking well over a hundred bucks for a decent seat.

I passed the world-famous "Welcome to Fabulous Las Vegas Nevada" sign. I noticed an Elvis impersonator working the crowd for tips. If you wanted your photo with Elvis, it would cost you a ten spot or maybe more. Another guy working the group was dressed as Big Bird.

I figured I was getting close to the batting cages place, but I didn't want to rush in cold turkey. I needed to think things over, balance the crazy books tumbling around in my head.

I pulled into a sandwich shop. I'd grab a bite to eat and get some coffee. I watched to see if anyone else drove into the parking lot after me. The lot had only a few cars. I parked near the door and waited a minute. No takers.

Inside, I sat alone in a booth facing the front door.

It had been a Hell of a day.

Dealing with Neal Braxton at the Galloping Dominos Casino had been like pulling teeth. I finally got a few still photos from Braxton of Ted Evans, Charlemagne's manager. Finding the bag of coins and the half pack of French cigarettes in the busted-up chair in the theatre was my own doing.

Now it was clear that I wasn't the only one looking for our friend Charlemagne. Agents Fitch and Rice, who claimed to be from a mysterious government agency, were on the trail. So were the two Russians who claimed they had a massive deal for Charlemagne in Moscow.

The most disturbing was the guy who ended up under a bus trying to grab the coins in the plastic bag. I thought they had been quarters until the guy at the Pinball Museum pointed out that the coins were tokens at a batting cage place just to the south of the airport.

The waitress brought some coffee and took my order.

I took the plastic bag out of my jacket pocket and spilled the coins onto the table. It turned out to be a mixed bag. Four quarters, four batting cage tokens, and four coins that looked foreign – all about the same size. I couldn't make out the language or even the lettering. Something Arabic?

I took out my iPhone and arranged a group photo of the dozen coins. Then I turned them over and shot their flip sides. I attached the two pictures to an email and hit send.

A minute later, my iPhone buzzed. The caller ID said, "World's Sexiest Blonde." I hit the answer button.

"Nick," the voice said. "You been in Vegas for one day, and you're down to your last three bucks? Is this some kinda cry for help?"

It was my wife, Dawn.

"Hey, Babe," I started, but got cut off.

"Someone important wants to say something," Dawn said.

It was the most beautiful female in the world, our two-year-old, Molly. She had it all down in one long burst of air. She loved her first day at Hebrew daycare, where they sang songs and ate macaroons. Tomorrow they were going to the zoo at Lincoln Park, where they were having breakfast with Seymour, the sun bear.

"The kid's having a better day than I'm having," I said when Dawn got back on the phone.

"What's with the photos of the coins?"

"Take a good look," I said. "I found them in a sack under a cushion at Galloping Dominos. At first, I thought they were quarters, but you can see for yourself."

"It looks Aramaic," she said. "Kind of crudely done, or maybe a variation. Mainly consonants. The style used in the Mediterranean about maybe 2700 years ago. Is there some kind of ancient show going on in Vegas? Christ, they do everything out there, even exhibit cadavers."

She was right. They did have a show about the human body that had cadavers in it. She was right about the Aramaic, too. I hadn't married any dummy. Dawn was born in Israel and had been on the staff at USC in their Middle East Studies department. These days she was working alongside Jacky's wife Muriel trying to separate phony artifacts from the real thing before they were acquired by several museums in Chicago.

I told her about the rest of my day.

Her reactions: Braxton was a jerk.

Jimmy Cox was a charmer.

Fitch and Rice were phonies, not to be trusted.

Cassandra Black was smart and connected.

The Russians were funny but also not to be trusted.

As to our man under the bus: "Look out," she said, "Those types usually travel in packs."

She had one more piece of advice.

"Go back to the hotel and get some rest," she said. "Take your blood pressure, and remember you have a beautiful daughter."

CHAPTER SIX

I left the restaurant and headed back to my hotel. I was tired. Thinking didn't come easy sitting in a greasy spoon drinking from a bottomless pot of coffee. Back at the hotel, I took out my portable blood pressure cuff, and to no surprise, found it was time to pop an amlodipine and cool it. Room service brought up a pot of herbal tea and a tropical fruit salad, and I was ready to relax.

I dialed Cassandra Black's cell phone.

"Nick, was that you who put that guy under the bus on Tropicana Avenue?" She asked.

"Now why would I do a thing like that?"

"You need to see my friend Roland at the jail tomorrow morning," she said. "He went to the morgue and found a business card on the guy from agents Fitch and Rice. He also found some coins on him. Roland says they look Egyptian or Arabic."

"Aramaic," I said.

"How'd you know that?" She asked.

"I emailed a photo of the coins to my wife. She says Aramaic."

"Dawn. How is she?"

"Keeping in shape chasing our two-year-old," I said.

"Molly. How nice," she said.

She told me how to meet Roland, and she rang off.

I took the bag of coins out of my pocket. Our man under the bus had been collecting them and had somewhere along the way run into agents Fitch and Rice.

Disappearing Act

I didn't think he was part of their act. He wouldn't need one of their calling cards if he was on their payroll. No, Fitch and Rice had probably leaned on the guy in their ham-handed way and given him one of their digital tracking cards to keep tabs on him.

The batting cage coins had me going, too. Did Ted Evans, Charlemagne's manager, hang out at the batting cages? I put it on my list to check it out after I saw Roland.

My thoughts were interrupted by a phone call from Jimmy Cox.

"Hey, after you left me at the sportsbook, I thought about the situation with Houdini or Mandrake," he said. "I think you need to lean on that goof, Neal Braxton. One of my banking contacts hinted that Braxton was way behind on his car and house payments. He was supposed to stroll in and pay some heavy bills."

"How heavy?" I asked.

"Fifty Gs. When I first heard it, I figured he was skimming off the top of the proceeds at the Casino. But as you know, that kind of help-your-self can get you a burial plot out in the desert. Maybe he cut a deal with the magician. Maybe he'd stall Jacky on the payments each month for a small piece of the rental bill. Meantime Charlemagne would keep most of the mil each month while he got ready to split."

"Pretty good reasoning," I said. "You figure that all out on your own?"

"Let's just say I'm sleeping with a lady news and entertainment editor. For some reason, we both like you. Damned if I can remember why."

"I'll catch up to you tomorrow," I said. "Let you know what I find."

"Meet me in the afternoon at my office," he said. "I've got some info on the Hawks at Montreal. You may want to invest."

He rang off.

I hit the shower for a steamy indulgence. About ten minutes into it, I pictured Lake Mead sinking to a new depth behind Hoover Dam. I was the one, I decided. I was a one-man water shortage, probably responsible for global warming and whatever oil shortage or oil glut was currently in vogue. All those goddamn politicians and all their solutions had it wrong. They needed to find me and get me to stop.

"Piss on them all," I growled at the steamed-up mirror. I wanted to sleep.

I turned off the lights and got in bed. I was out in seconds.

There's probably some think tank somewhere studying the effects of drinking a pot of herbal tea before hitting the rack. Four hours into my sleep, I was up and running to the john. I had to pee, big time.

I came back out of the bathroom and headed back toward the bed when I noticed something was out of whack. I had put the stuff from my pants and jacket on the coffee table. I looked closer. The four Aramaic coins were casting a blue glow.

Just then, my cell phone rang.

"Nick, it's Cassandra. Neal Braxton's been shot dead."

CHAPTER SEVEN

I drove through the three am. traffic, which in Vegas looks a lot like the three pm. traffic, only the morning version is dark and more alcohol fueled.

Braxton's home was on Dunes Beach Drive, which sounds like it belongs on the North Carolina Outer Banks, among windswept dunes. In truth, it was just another street in the desert full of expensive homes on a golf course.

Braxton had bought it near the front door of his house in South Vegas, a separate town just outside Vegas. You could call it a suburb, but that could get you dirty looks from South Vegas folks. It was one of the fastest growing towns in Nevada, rivaling Vegas and, according to some, offering better housing and shopping.

Cassandra Black said I'd get cooperation from Detective Jake Glover of the South Vegas PD. He'd be at the scene looking for clues and mopping up what was left of Neal Braxton.

Glover had no trouble accepting me into the fold once I dropped Cassandra's name. He was a beat-up looking guy in his mid-fifties who would never have a drinking problem as long as he had a few drinks. I figured he knew how to play the game. Cassandra had the guy on speed dial.

"You're the guy out of Chicago," he said. "Cassandra says you're trying to find the magician that took off. Good luck with that one."

"Yeah, Charlemagne," I said. "You ever catch his act?"

"Shit," he said. "Do I look like Wayne Newton to you? I only meet guys like that when they step out of line or end up dead like this one." He pointed to the sheet covering Neal Braxton.

I asked him how it went down.

"Pretty basic," he said. "There's his car in the drive. He stepped out of it, went toward the door, someone caught his attention and put three slugs into him. I figure a revolver. No shell casings left behind."

Braxton's Escalade was still running in the driveway. The driver's side door hung open. An alarm from the car verified that the door was hanging open. It was no doubt sending a message to Detroit that the door was open. There was probably a message on Braxton's phone that the door was open. Despite all the effort, Braxton wasn't getting up to close it.

Maybe he was trying to get to his house to pick something up. Maybe he meant to run out again. He never made it.

"We got the call about an hour ago," Glover said. "I phoned our lady friend right away so she could get a reporter and a photographer out here. She appreciates a heads-up on stories like that. That's when she told me that you might be showing up."

He nodded toward a young guy taking pictures of the car. Next to him stood a slim brunette writing down Braxton's plate number.

I figured Jake Glover was getting money in an envelope for steering Cassandra toward good crime stories. He was for sale. The question was, for how much?

"You figure he was trying to run into the house for something and run out again?" I asked.

"I'd bet a c-note on it," Glover said.

"I'd bet two," I said, handing him two Ben Franklins. "Let's take a look."

The house was large, five bedrooms, two great rooms, a pool in the back yard, and a three-car garage attached to the house. It was also damn near empty. A card table stood in the middle of the first great room. A plastic chair was next to it. A cheap laptop was on the table next to cold coffee in a paper cup. In the corner of the room was an inflatable bed. It was unmade.

Glover stood there, laughing.

"Your high and your mighty," he said. "Goddamn town's full of phonies. I bet the house is foreclosed. Looks like maybe he's been selling off the contents before they toss him out."

I touched the space bar on the computer. It came to life on a Craigslist page that had Braxton's ads listed. I pulled a flash drive out of my pocket and held it up to Glover. He nodded.

"Go ahead, it's your nickel," he said.

In minutes I had the contents of Braxton's computer on the flash drive. Our search of the rest of his house revealed a lot of empty dirty space. His closet had several changes of clothes, and the kitchen was a collection of trash from different carry-out places. Toss in your necessary grooming supplies, and that was it.

The Escalade was more of the same - soft drink empties, hamburger wrappers, and a couple of combs.

I asked Glover what he had found on Braxton's body.

"His wallet had ten bucks in it," he said. "There were a few quarters, maybe a couple bucks worth. Take a look,"

He dumped them into my hand.

"They're all yours," he said.

I figured Glover had done a wallet-ectomy on Braxton and had scored enough to keep the whiskey flowing for some time. I grabbed the coins and stepped over to the kitchen sink, where there was an over-the-counter light: seven quarters, two batting cage tokens, one Aramaic coin.

I shoved the coins into my pocket and went back to where Glover was standing.

"You don't have a couple of birds named Fitch and Rice on your speed dial, do you?" I asked.

"Those two assholes," he said. "They want everything for free. I heard they even tried to cheat a working gal. They're usually about three lengths behind the field."

I told Glover I'd be in touch and got into my rental. As I eased away from the curb, I noticed a grey sedan pull up and stop in front of the dearly departed Neal Braxton's home. If it wasn't the team known as Fitch and Rice getting out of the car, it was a damn good imitation.

CHAPTER EIGHT

I couldn't take the chance that Fitch and Rice had made the plate on my rental car as they pulled up in front of the late Neal Braxton's abode. I drove to Avis and exchanged the red Ford Fusion for a blue Nissan Sentra. I hoped that whoever rented the Fusion that day would drive it to someplace like Needles with agents Fitch and Rice on their tail.

I went back to the hotel. I got a couple hours of shuteye and ordered breakfast from room service.

It was too early to meet Roland at the jail, so I plugged the info from Braxton's laptop into mine using the flash drive. The Craigslist page wasn't much of a surprise. He had sold off most of the furnishings in the house along with several flat screens, a motorbike, and a jet ski.

If he got half of what he was asking for the stuff, he would have cleared over 30 grand. You couldn't stuff that into your wallet. Somewhere there was a roll, and I didn't think Detective Glover had it. His type was more into grabbing out of the wallet and taking a Rolex off the vic's wrist.

Maybe there were more than 30 Gs. If Braxton was taking a fee each month from Charlemagne to stall Jacky on the monthly rent for the theater, there had to be over a hundred grand. Unless it went up Braxton's nose.

Maybe Jimmy Cox didn't have the whole story about Braxton owing 50 Gs on the house and car. But Jimmy had a lot of it right. From the looks of the home on Dunes Beach Drive,

Braxton wasn't trying to hang on there. He was in the process of taking it on the lam.

I phoned Jacky in Chicago to tell him of the sudden demise of Neal Braxton. He didn't seem surprised.

"I'm surprised he's lived this long," Jacky said. "Son of a bitch never could keep his act straight. I told the Feldsteins when they bought the Dominos that they should keep an eye on him. When I took the long-term lease on the theatre, I thought their accountant would handle the collections. Next thing, she's quit, and that asshole's in charge."

I gave him a quick rundown on my first day in Sin City and told him I'd be following up on a few of our friends to see what help they might be.

"Jesus," he said. "Watch your ass, Nick. I don't want to deal with Dawn if you end up under the bus."

He rang off.

I was back into the cyber world of Neal Braxton. His favorite websites dealt with fast cars, drugs, and guns. His email consisted of come-ons from crossdressers and car dealers and threatening notices from bill collectors. My guess was that the computer on his desk at the casino was more business-like. I'd find a way to look at that one.

I wanted to get back into Braxton's house to do more digging. Detective Glover figured the crime scene was just the front lawn where Braxton caught a quick dose of lead poisoning. Glover was disappointed when we walked into the nearly empty house. Everything grab-able had already been grabbed. His crime lab boys had done a quick once-over of the Escalade and the front lawn and went off to a shooting and home invasion on Water Street.

The early morning TV news had the Braxton shooting along with the one on Water Street as lead stories. Still, it soon gave way to a story about a couple getting arrested for having sex on the 500-foot-tall Ferris wheel just off the strip. Now there was a couple with all heart but no business sense, I thought. In Vegas, you charge for performances like that. Giving it away only gets you arrested.

The Ferris wheel sex story gave way to one speculating among bookies as to the odds of the Oakland Raiders moving to

Vegas. There was a match made in heaven, I thought. The books, though, weren't acting like angels. They were accusing each other of giving false odds on the Raiders arriving in Sin City.

Then there was a live update from the scene at Water Street, which proved to be nowhere near any water. They should have called it Desert Street. A late-breaking story came after that about a Black male found shot to death inside a car on Cindysue Street in central Las Vegas Valley. The reporter stood in front of a dumpy house that looked like the one on Water Street. Who in the Hell, I wondered, would do a thing like that – name a street "Cindysue?"

Nowhere was there any mention of my guy who got squished under the tour bus on Tropicana. For a minute, I thought of calling the station and complaining.

I could hear myself running the riot act to some flunky at TV 20.

"Hey this is Nick. What happened to the redneck I saw go under the bus in front of the Pinball Hall of Fame? Wasn't that story good enough for you?"

I decided against it. It wasn't the kind of thing you could take pride in. Dawn would be pissed if I did something like that.

I thought of our two-year-old Molly. Later today she'd be visiting Lincoln Park Zoo to see Seymour the sun bear. I could be proud of her.

On the coffee table, the Aramaic coins were no longer glowing. Daylight had come.

The jail was located on Casino Center Boulevard. The Vegas experience reminded me of a massive Monopoly game. If you crapped out on the strip, you might get sent to the conveniently located county jail. You didn't pass go or collect 200 bucks, but you would view some colorful bail bond signs on your way to the grey bar hotel.

The office sign said, "Governor's Office of Rehabilitation and Enquiry, Roland Rivers, Deputy-in-charge."

His outer office had six people in cubicles. Everyone was on the phone except the receptionist. She was a slim, well-dressed woman of about forty who asked me if I was Mr. Nick from Chicago.

Before I could mumble an answer, she said, "Go right on in, Mr. Rivers is expecting you."

He was a slim, dark-haired guy in his late thirties. He wore a white polo shirt with blue slacks. A plastic ID hung from a chain around his neck. I would have bet Latino. Turned out, I would have won.

"Roland Rivers," he said. He stood to shake my hand. "Rolando Rivera, before I changed it before I came out here. My family has the Conchita Restaurant on 16th Street in the Pilsen section of Chicago. You maybe heard of my old man, Ernesto Rivera, the alderman?"

I had heard of his old man. The locals along 16th Street called him by his nickname "Neto." Neto had come up through the ranks at the plumbers union before he ran for the city council. He was one of the first to send his election workers to Iowa on behalf of then-Senator Obama. Was Neto connected? Do the Bears play in Soldier Field?

We sat. The receptionist brought coffee. We talked about the Blackhawks kicking ass, the Bears getting their ass kicked, and the Cubs and the Sox waiting until next year to get their asses kicked. He asked about Jacky.

"Jacky's fine," I said. "Minus a few million bucks the magician made off with."

"Hell of a story," Roland said. "And now Braxton's on a slab, and you slipped some redneck under a bus. Jesus, Nick. You hit the town, and things start to happen."

"I only take partial credit," I said. "Next they'll be blaming me for that couple doing the dirty on the Ferris wheel."

"I hear that sex on the wheel is pretty common," he said.

"What you do in Vegas stays in Vegas," I said.

He reached into his center desk drawer and pulled out a small plastic bag. He tossed it onto the desk toward me. There were four Aramaic coins, a couple quarters, and a raised letter business card from Agent Rice.

"Jeff Davis," he said. "That's your mug from under the bus. Once upon a time fullback for Ole Miss, ex green beret, three-time divorcee, multiple wife-beater and DOA under the Vegas Exotic Nightlife Tour Bus. I was able to get these from our law enforcement pipeline. They're all yours."

Disappearing Act

I looked at the coins.

"This was all he had on him?"

"He had his Florida Driver's License and a pretty empty wallet. Needless to say, some of our people tend to help themselves."

"I'm shocked. Not in Sin City."

"Hey, you forget," he said. "Some of the people who wrote the rules book in this town started out in Chicago."

"Any idea who Jeff Davis was connected with?" I asked. "Didn't he used to be President of the Confederacy?"

"Hey, for all we know, he could be working with Robert E. Lee." Roland said. "Vegas attracts guys like that. They all think they're Rambo. A bunch of stumblebums who think their mission from God is to recover OJ's memorabilia. We have some of them as guests here in jail. Some of them never make it that far. They have heart attacks in whorehouses out in the desert."

"Classy way to go," I said. "No doubt big items in the society pages."

"Better than under a fuckin' tour bus," he said.

He handed me a copy of Jeff Davis's rap sheet.

We talked a few minutes more. His office, which he referred to as GORE – Governor's Office of Rehabilitation and Enquiry, was basically a place to stash pay rollers who could get out the vote. All the phone conversations I had witnessed on the way in had something to do with dispensing political favors or receiving them.

Now that we had received some help from Roland on the Charlemagne problem, one of Neto's people would be suggesting a lunch out with Jacky. They would talk about the next big campaign and the high cost of getting the message out.

Jacky rarely donated money to campaigns. He'd respond by giving beer and booze from the distributorship he owned. Politics in Chicago ran on high-test alcohol.

We exchanged cellphone numbers, and I left.

I wanted to get to Galloping Dominos Casino to check out Braxton's office. Jacky had said he'd have the way cleared for me with Jerry Feldstein, one of the partners.

I pulled away from the jail and headed for the strip. Behind me in a red Mustang convertible were two familiar faces, the

Russian tag-team of Boris and Alexi. I pulled over to the side and put my flashers on. They pulled up behind and stopped.

I walked back to see if I could help two lost tourists.

"You boys looking for a good time?" I asked. "Did you wear out that whorehouse you're hanging out at?"

They ignored my charming repartee and plunged into their own rap.

"Is too bad about friend Neal Braxton," Boris said from behind the steering wheel.

"Yeah, a real shame," I said. "You boys didn't have any part in his demise, did you?"

"Nyet, we friends," Alexi said. "Now make harder to find magician, no?"

"I'm still looking, but if I were you, boys, I wouldn't follow me right now," I said. "I just came from the jail. Some people from Immigration were asking if I knew anything about two Russians. I told them, no, but I'm thinking the feds might be following me."

Boris quickly backed the Mustang away from my Nissan and swung off into traffic.

I could hear Alexi yell, *"Da svedanya."* He waved his hand, and they were soon out of sight.

CHAPTER NINE

As I drove toward the Galloping Dominos Casino, I thought about what I knew so far. Several people were after Charlemagne, but not all were after him for the same reason. I figured agents Fitch and Rice wanted him for what he knew and the equipment he used in his show. The Russians were after him for the same reason. However, I could see some Moscow Circus extravaganza as part of their motivation.

I was after him for the money. In fact, I didn't care who had the money. If he had paid it to Braxton and I somehow found it, it was case closed. Nick would be back in Chicago sitting at center ice at the Blackhawks games with a gorgeous blonde wife at his side.

Well, it wasn't quite that cut and dried.

I had to be honest with myself. The glowing Aramaic coins, being attacked by Jeff Davis at the Pinball Machine Hall of Fame, Braxton getting offed, and the mysterious Ted Evans made me want to dig deeper. Money was only part of what was at the end of this rainbow. Some people were after more.

Apparently, Detective Glover was too hung-over. So, the South Vegas PD sent Detective Tom Duffy to the Galloping Dominos Casino to see what could be learned about the demise of Neal Braxton. Duffy was a skinny, freckle-faced kid about twenty-three who could have passed as a youth worker at the YMCA.

He had called ahead, making appointments with Jerry Feldstein and his wife, Marcy. Jerry was supposedly in charge of the place now that Braxton was dead. Proving himself a suitable replacement for Braxton, Jerry ducked out of the interview with Duffy to go play golf with a nightclub owner from Detroit.

I got there as Duffy was finishing up with Marcy.

"So, Mrs. Feldstein," he said. "As far as you know, there was no one here at the casino who was at odds with Mr. Braxton?"

"No," she said, looking over Duffy's shoulder at me standing in the doorway to her office. "He was highly thought of by the staff. Neal was a lot of fun to be around. This had to be something else. There're so many maniacs out on the streets with guns. Poor Neal."

Duffy left.

Marcy motioned for me to come in.

"Close the door, Nick," she said. "Jacky says you were at the scene late last night."

"More like three this morning," I said. "Detective Jake Glover was at the scene with some of the forensics crew from Henderson.

"Glover," she said, rolling her eyes. "Never turned down a drink."

"It looks like Braxton was getting ready to run, Marcy. The house was empty, and his laptop looked like it was married to Craigslist."

"You think he was embezzling?"

"I don't know what he had access to here. He might have been taking a cut from Charlemagne's people to stall Jacky from getting the rent on the theatre. Or maybe he pocketed it all. In that case, I don't need to find Charlemagne. I just need to find the money."

Marcy leaned back in her chair and put the tips of her fingers together. Her nails were manicured and polished, but not in any flamboyant Vegas way. She was dressed for doing serious business in a navy-blue suit with one string of pearls.

"Braxton was a jerk, Nick," she said. "We watched him pretty close. Most of our billing is in plastic. We caught him a few times dipping into petty cash, but he brought in a decent crowd of spenders, so we let it go. A few hundred here and there – we thought of it as vig. Hell, Jerry drops that playing golf sometimes. He's another one I keep my eyes on."

She was in charge. Art Feldstein, her father-in-law, owned the Galloping Dominos Casino. He bought it after Jacky had purchased the liquor distributorship in Chicago from Art and his brother Harry.

Harry just wanted his money from the booze company so he could retire to Miami. Art had just enough to make it in Vegas. That's when Jacky stepped in to help by taking the long-term lease on the theatre.

At first, Art tried to mold his son Jerry into being boss. He would have been good at it if the job had been playing golf and getting drunk with customers, but that wasn't going to cut it. Marcy stepped up with her business degree from Northwestern and her family connections. Being a daughter of Sammy Di Carlo, owner of Black Like Me Records and Country Cussin' Records, had taught her that robbing Jamal to pay Daisy Mae was a standard business practice. Braxton and Jerry had fancy titles, but Marcy held the ends of their leashes.

In short, she was made for Vegas.

I put the plastic bag with the four Aramaic coins and the two quarters on the desk.

"You ever see any of these?" I asked.

She looked at them closely and shook her head.

"Odd lettering," she said. "Hebrew?"

"Aramaic," I said.

"How'd you know that?" She asked.

"I have a smart wife."

"Ah, yes. Dawn. How is she?"

It was a question with a cold front approaching.

"Beautiful and smarter than ever," I said.

"How nice," she said. "What exactly are they?"

"Something people are willing to die for, apparently."

"You find these where?"

"In the theatre. On the guy who ran under the bus."

"That was your doing?" She asked.

"I was trying to stop him," I said. "He was trying to rob me."

She nodded and took a sip from her water bottle.

"Do you think Ted Evans has something to do with these?"

"Evans ever smoke cigarettes around you?" I asked.

"Yeah, some French brand," she said.

"I found one of these coins on our friend Neal Braxton," I said.

"It's hard to see Braxton involved in anything with Ted Evans," she said.

"I got the impression from Braxton that he didn't think much of Evans," I said.

She laughed and shook her head.

Braxton's office revealed nothing. He had barely touched his computer. His desk was nearly empty except for brochures and local magazines. His civic awards and pictures of him with various celebrities hung on the wall.

"Not much here to go on," I said.

"That's who he was," Marcy said. "Not much there at all. Everyone here thought he was a shit."

CHAPTER TEN

"Work your precincts."
You hear that in Chicago. Usually, it's one politician to another. It means get off your butt and find out what your voters are thinking. Listen. You might learn something.

And it works better if you dress to fit in. A three-piece suit won't work in a grease monkey bar.

Dick's Sporting Goods had what I needed. I bought an aluminum bat, and a Chicago Cubs shirt that hung over my waist covering the Glock I had stuck in the back of my pants. A baseball cap with some wild sport shades completed the outfit.

I was ready to hang out at the batting cages and see what I could shake loose. For a guy over fifty, I'm in good shape. I know baseball and all its varieties, most of which are found in Chicago and some almost nowhere else.

There's softball, the 12-inch variety, played with gloves. It can either be slow pitch or fast. Then there's the fourteen-inch variety, which most people outside Chicago have never seen. The fourteen-inch type has raised seams that stick out of the ball about an eighth of an inch. A good fourteen-inch pitcher will tell you he can do boomerangs with the ball. This claim has never been documented. But is frequently sworn to and at by batters who have tried to hit against such a pitcher. A barrel of beer on the premises during the game has something to do with the claims and counterclaims.

There's also a sixteen-inch variety. No gloves, but plenty of excitement caused by the barrel of beer and a few near heart attacks from the 85-year-old players who still think they can run like teenagers.

I carried my new bat into the Feel Da Dreams batting cage complex just south of the airport. It was an exciting place with about a dozen cages. You could hit against a 30 mph 12-inch softball toss or go all the way up to the 80 mph—hardball pitching. The place was a stadium with a distance of 350 feet to the outfield walls.

Behind the counter sat a tall blonde dressed in a softball uniform- red top with blue lettering in neon sign type, "Vegas Dykes."

"You the owner?" I asked.

"Shit, don't I wish," she said. "I watch the place during the day. Sometimes I get a few swings in to keep in shape. My team has games in the evenings. It's usually cooler then."

"So, you play in a league?"

"Yeah, slow-pitch mixed league," she said. "Supposed to have men and women on each team, but we're all women. They let us slide through. We tell them some of us are having sex changes. When we're done, we promise to show everyone our new dicks."

I laughed.

"Jesus, that's a great story," I said.

"Yeah, after 'don't ask, don't tell' and all the other shit that was supposed to make everyone feel comfortable, I'm happy to be out and talking about it."

Her name was Karen. She told me the Vegas Dykes were playing at a local park that night. I wrote down the directions on a slip of paper.

"You gonna hit some balls?"

"Yeah, in Chicago, I play on a tavern team, the Old Town Maniacs. Twelve-inch slow pitch. A bunch of lawyers and dentists. I figure I'm out here for a few days, so it might be fun to hit a few. Someone told me an old cowboy named Zeke recommended this place, so I thought I'd come by and take a few swings. Big guy with a huge beard."

"I know him," she said. "He's the one with the bat. Hasn't been around in a while. He's some kind of inventor."

"Didn't know that," I said.

"Yeah, but I don't think he'd ever get it approved for play in any organized league," she said. "It's a bat that you can put different settings on."

I must have looked puzzled.

"It's made out of some kind of composite material," she said. The knob on the end of the bat can be turned for the different settings."

"And what does that get you?" I asked.

"One thing it does, it makes the ball skip radically sideways after it hits the dirt. You can set it for left or right, and it flies off at about a 30-degree angle from where the ball hits. It also puts a radical backspin on the ball, so it stops dead like on a billiard table, and then it backs up from where it hit."

"I never heard of anything like that," I said. "Did you try it?"

"Couple times," she said. "Real high-tech stuff, though. You could tell by the feel of it that it would be way too expensive for the average player to have. The real bitch is fly balls. You can set the bat, so the balls drop at a 45-degree angle. If you pop up to the shortstop, the ball ends up falling in right field somewhere."

"Hell, that happens all the time in Chicago if you play along the lakefront," I said.

We both laughed.

"Well," I said. "Better give me a ten-dollar treatment. Maybe I can hit a few singles."

She handed me a plastic cup full of batting cage tokens. They looked like the ones I had already found since arriving in Vegas.

I got my swings in at the softball cages and then took on the 80 mph fastballs. I finally got a few foul tips in as my ten bucks came to a close.

I waved to Karen on my way out.

"How'd it go?" She asked.

"Had a good time," I said. "Might catch your game later."

I got to the car and found my phone. There was a message from Dawn. A video opened, revealing an unforgettable couple. Our two-year-old Molly was standing in front of a fence pointing at Seymour, the sun bear behind bars. A keeper stood near

Disappearing Act

Seymour feeding him what I could only guess was the sun bear equivalent of a power lunch. Seymour was doing his best to put the food all over the Walter Payton Bears jersey he wore. As the camera lens panned left, it was evident that Seymour was vastly outnumbered by a couple dozen two-year-olds screaming their asses off. Seymour was a big hit.

I rang Dawn's phone.

"Did you see Molly with Seymour?" She asked.

"He's cute, but I don't want to adopt him," I said. "What the hell were they feeding him?"

"Ground up Green Bay Packer, the zookeeper told us," she said. "How you doing out there?"

I told her about Braxton getting shot, meeting Detective Glover, and later meeting Roland at the jail.

"He's the son of Ernesto Rivera, the alderman," I said.

"I know Ernesto's wife, Gloria," Dawn said. "She's on the advisory board at the Clark Museum."

"Small world," I said.

I told her about meeting with Marcy Feldstein at the Galloping Dominos and how Jerry Feldstein bowed out of the meeting with the South Vegas PD to play golf with a nightclub owner from Detroit.

"That Jerry's a real piece of work, Nick," she said. "One of the main reasons they sold the liquor business to Jacky was because Harry Feldstein couldn't stand to be around Jerry. Muriel told me all about it over lunch one day at the Drake. Art tried to get Jacky and Muriel to keep his son Jerry on at the company after they bought it, but Muriel put her foot down."

"I've seen her do that," I said.

"She told Jacky she didn't want that jerk around the business," Dawn said.

"So that's how he ended up at Galloping Dominos," I said. "Was Braxton part of Jerry's circle in Chicago?"

"They knew each other. Don't know how, but they went out boozing together, according to Muriel. They used to hang out at a place called Mister Freddie's."

"Charlemagne's manager Ted Evans is a philosopher. Apparently, he talks about righteousness coming out of the clouds in the desert and trying to get people to look at things in a different way

"He's the guy with the beard?"

"Yeah, I tracked him to the Feel Da Dreams batting cages. Turns out he's an inventor. I didn't see him, but I heard about his crazy bat that does strange things to a baseball. Puts English on the ball. It hits the ground and takes off wildly. Those were his coins, the ones I found at the theatre with the French cigarettes."

"Oh, the Aramaic coins, Nick," she said. "The inscription on them says 'Ezekiel' like the prophet in the Bible. He prophesized visions coming out of the clouds."

"Yeah," I said. "And Evans refers to himself as Old Zeke."

CHAPTER ELEVEN

"And I looked, and behold, a whirlwind came out of the north, a great cloud, and a fire in-folding itself, and a brightness was about it, and out of the midst thereof as the color of amber, out of the midst of the fire. Also, out of the midst thereof came the likeness of four living creatures. And this was their appearance; they had the likeness of a man. And everyone had four faces, and everyone had four wings."

It was an email from Dawn. Actually, it was from the original Ezekiel forwarded from Dawn. Marry an expert on the Middle East, and you'll never guess which prophet's message she may deliver to you. It could be Moses discussing Jehovah or Sid from Sheridan Road Dry Cleaners telling you your suit is ready to be picked up.

The original Ezekiel sounded a lot like Old Zeke, the cowboy. If anyone was guilty of plagiarism, the old cowboy would take the fall. I was on my way to meet Jimmy Cox at the sports betting joint. As far as I could tell, neither agents Fitch and Rice nor the Russian tag team of Alexi and Boris were on my tail. Having cleared that mental concern, Dawn's warning about Jeff Davis types traveling in packs came to mind. Would someone from the Ole Miss alumni association show up to get the Aramaic coins from me? Would they all be over-weight drunks? Did they all have a penchant for running into the street in front of tour buses?

You couldn't figure it out. You had to live it.

You also couldn't figure out the hot tip Jimmy Cox had on the Blackhawks vs. the Canadiens.

"Christ sakes, listen this time, will ya," he said for maybe the fifth time. "If the Hawks are ahead by two or more goals toward the end of the game, Montreal will pull its goalie for another forward. If they do it before the two minutes left to play mark and they don't score, we get four-to-one odds. If there's a penalty and both the Hawks player and the Canadiens player go for two minutes, we get eight-to-one odds. If the Canadiens score a goal, it goes to sixteen-to-one. If the Hawks score an empty-net goal, we get thirty-two-to one. Now, if the puck..."

That was as far as I could follow him. Somehow for a c-note, I'd either go down the drain or end up owning half of Quebec. It was easier to hand him the money and take him to a late lunch.

We ate at a place that specialized in ribs and coleslaw. Both may have been the best I ever tasted. There were pictures of entertainers all over the walls. Siegfried and Roy hung next to Mac King, who hung next to Penn and Teller on the Magicians Row. Celine hung next to Cher on Singers Row. Joe Williams, the jazz singer who was with Count Basie, hung above our table. I thought about Williams, one of Sinatra's favorite singers. He died after he wandered away from his home in Vegas. He was a confused old man, far from the lively singer of "Every Day I Have the Blues," depicted in the photo.

"So, what can I help you with?" Jimmy brought me out of my séance with Joe Williams.

"I'm thinking the money is one thing," I said. "Finding Charlemagne and his cohorts may be another issue altogether."

"So, whoever has the money may not be Charlemagne, but whatever Charlemagne has that people are after is something else? Like the secret of how his show works?"

"Yeah, maybe the equipment."

"I saw the show once with Cassandra," Jimmy said. "It was another world. You thought you were in one of those special effects movies. I was a little dizzy walking out of there."

He took a swig out of his beer bottle.

"Here's the thing, Nick. The money is the two million owed to Jacky. If Charlemagne kept it, he's the one to go looking for, but there's something not kosher about it. The guy's got the hottest show on the strip, and according to Neal Braxton, he wants to renegotiate his deal with Jacky for less rent. So instead, he disappears? Shit. With a hot act like that, he'd be out taking bids from a dozen casinos. He wouldn't just go off and disappear. Plus, he'd be talking with Jacky about more seats in the theatre, special shows. You know how it works."

"Yeah, I know how it works," I said. "So, let's say Braxton pocketed the two mil. Why does Charlemagne disappear? He'd be thinking that Jacky was getting the rent money, and everything on that front would be okay, no?"

"Unless Braxton gets wind of the fact that Charlemagne's got to leave soon for some reason or other and ..."

"And it's now or never if Braxton wants his piece of the action," I finished Jimmy's sentence. "He figures he gets two-month's rent out of the magician before he blows town, and everyone figures that Charlemagne took the dough with him when he left."

Jimmy put down the rib he was chewing on and wiped his hands.

"So, let's say Braxton has the two mil and he's behind on the mortgage and his car payment like I heard. Only instead of paying off his bills, he decides to run with the dough. How would you do it, Nick?"

"Braxton had to make some contacts while he was at the Galloping Dominos," I said. "If I'm him, I got people in Mexico where I can drive the Escalade and drop it in a chop shop for a good price. This gets me the option of working my way south to one of the small resorts or even farther to Panama or Costa Rica. I've got two mil plus whatever I got from selling off all the shit at the house, maybe another forty or fifty thousand in cash."

"Yeah," Jimmy said. "It all works for him until someone decides to plug him on his front lawn, which happens the day you get into town and tell him Jacky wants his dough. The question is, 'was he plugged on the way into the house, or on the way out'?"

I sat silent for a while, thinking. If someone grabbed the money from Braxton after shooting him as he left his house, it was someone who knew what he was up to, someone who knew he was stealing and getting ready to run.

"Was it someone who was in on it with him? Someone afraid of being double-crossed?" I asked.

"Maybe," Jimmy said. "On the other hand, maybe he gets shot running to his house for cover. Someone's following him.

They get a little excited and pop off three rounds at Braxton. It's way too loud for that neighborhood. They take off into the night."

"He was running toward the house," I said. "His car door was hanging open, and the 'door open' alarm was on. You don't let that happen if you're trying to make a quick and quiet getaway."

Jimmy chewed on another rib and looked up at me.

"You were in that house with what's his name? The happy hour detective, yeah?"

"Glover," I said. "We gave it the once over search. Not much in the place."

"We should go back in," Jimmy said. "We'll take some tools and take the place apart."

Jimmy had a labyrinth for a brain. It was no surprise that we'd start our search of Neal Braxton's house by invading the office of the guy who owned the rib place.

"This is Gus," Jimmy said as he sat looking at the computer on Gus's desk. "Gus comes from a good family. His people used to run the Club Diamond in McHenry. They sold the place just before the fire and came out here."

You could rack your brain trying to figure out where McHenry was or what happened to the Club Diamond or what the fire was all about, but it wouldn't get you anywhere. You were better off saying, 'Oh, Yeah, pleased to meet you,' and moving on.

Gus mentioned that he knew Jacky and Muriel and that they had eaten at the rib place; they were good people, and whatever he could do to help us, he would do. We ran through the litany of what was wrong with the Bears, how the Cubs were only a steady reliever away from taking it all, and how the Chicago winters were just too damn cold.

I used my talent for nodding and saying, "Damn right!" a few times, and we were soon long-lost friends.

"Okay, I Googled everything we need to know, and I have a fix on some of the properties adjacent to Braxton's," Jimmy said. "Gus, can we get a half dozen of those plastic gloves you guys use in the food prep? We don't want to leave traces of barbecue sauce on anything we touch."

Gus laughed and went to get the plastic gloves.

"Nice guy, good people," Jimmy said. "He bought us lunch. You better bless the waitress on the way out."

We said goodbye to Gus. I slipped the waitress a couple of twenties, and we headed out the door. My afternoon with Jimmy had so far cost me a hundred and forty bucks. I had an undecipherable bet on the Blackhawks and a "free" lunch to show for it.

CHAPTER TWELVE

Jimmy had a vintage Cadillac El Dorado. It was big enough to have its own zip code. We stood in the parking lot at Ribs by Gus digging through the trunk, trying to find what Jimmy said was an essential part of getting into Braxton's house.

He found what he was looking for under a set of golf clubs. The two magnetic signs read, "Butch Cassidy Realty."

"This will work," he said, hanging one on each of the front doors. "Get in. We're going to visit the Braxton digs, but we'll be entering from the golf course side."

I sunk into the plush seat that only a Caddy of a particular vintage can offer. Floating on a cloud comes close to describing it.

We rode along. A thought surfaced.

"Real estate?" I asked. "I thought you weren't supposed to do legal work as part of your agreement to retire?"

"Yeah, that's true," Jimmy said. "But it's real estate. There's nothing legal about it. I show a few houses and take my cut when they sell."

I couldn't resist.

"Nothing legal?"

"You know what I mean," Jimmy said. "It's not like I'm saving some perp from doing eight to ten on a robbery rap. I'm trying to ease some goof into his dream condo."

"Butch Cassidy Realty?" I asked. "Why didn't you go all the way and call yourself Sundance Realty?"

"I thought of that," he said. "I didn't want to get Cassandra pissed at me. We go up to the film festival in Park City every year. We've met Redford a few times. Nice guy. Besides, some shmuck was trying to register that name at the time, but I think he went broke."

"We've been driving past streets named Wigwam and Windmill," I said. "It makes me think I'm on the world's biggest miniature golf layout. I figure Butch Cassidy Realty isn't too far out of line."

"You know there's a Dan Blocker street in Vegas, don't you?" Jimmy asked.

"Yeah, so what?" I said. "There's a Cindysue Street, too. I hear someone whacked one of the brothers there last night in front of a four-star crack house."

"It's obvious to me that you don't care about high culture," Jimmy said. "You have no idea who Dan Blocker was, do you?"

"No, and you probably don't either," I said. "But you're going to tell me some bullshit about him being some well-hung porn star. You're gonna say there's a Dan Tackler, too."

We stopped at a red light where traffic was tied up. Jimmy looked at me as if I were a cop on the witness stand who had just admitted to planting false evidence.

"You never heard of Bonanza?" He asked. "Dan Blocker played one of the lead roles. He was Hoss."

"That must have been my night to go to the opera," I said.

He looked at me again and saw me trying to stop a smirk from turning into a laugh.

"Nick, you son of a bitch," he said.

We both burst out laughing.

"Jesus! Your night at the fucking opera." Jimmy shook his head and drove on.

Braxton's house backed up onto a gated golf course. You could enter his home from the street side without going through a gate, but there was crime scene tape all over the lawn and driveway, and you'd be seen going in. If you wanted to drive into the golf course side, you had to go through an electronically keyed gate.

Jimmy had it figured, though. We pulled off to the side of the gate and waited for a car to arrive for entry. A Mercedes approached. Before the car got to the gate, we jumped out of the Cadillac and waved the car down.

"Hey, that guy Jose or Julio that works the desk at the golf club gave me a code for the gate, but it doesn't work," Jimmy said to the grey-haired woman driving the Mercedes. "I have this client here from Chicago who wants to see some of the properties. Can you help me out?"

She looked at us standing there and took a drag on her extra-long cigarette.

Jimmy looked the part of a realtor in his golf shirt and slacks. I had Chicago labels all over me – a Cubs hat and shirt, which even had a few barbecue stains on it. How authentic, I thought. If she wanted any more Chicago proof, I would have been happy to pull the Glock out of the back of my pants and wave it around.

"Follow me in," she said. "Those goddamn wetbacks can't even count straight."

We followed her in and turned off into the driveway of a house that had a for sale sign. There were no curtains. The late afternoon sun poured through the windows. It was empty and looked like no one had been around it in weeks.

"This one's a bank repo. It's across the fairway from Braxton's," Jimmy said.

We stopped and went to the trunk. The golf bag had what we needed, according to Jimmy. I grabbed it, and we headed across the fairway.

There was a wooden privacy fence separating Braxton's swimming pool from the fairway. It was open on both ends of the property line. The pool pump was on, and everything outside looked clean. There were two lounge chairs side-by-side. The rest of the backyard was vacant. No locker, no gas grill, no pool toys.

I motioned Jimmy toward a staircase that led to the second-floor balcony.

"When I was here last night, I left the door up there unlocked," I said.

He grabbed the golf bag and went up the stairs. I followed him through the door to what was once the master bedroom. Now it was just empty dirty space.

"You gotta look for panels and a/c ducts that can be opened," he said. "Sometimes, there's a panel in the ceiling leading to the attic."

We looked. No duct had been opened since it had been painted over years ago. There was no secret passage to the attic. The fridge and the dishwasher were gone. There was no washer and no dryer. The laptop still stood on the card table with the white plastic chair next to it. Jimmy looked under the inflatable bed. Nothing.

We looked in toilet tanks, under sinks. Nothing.

Now we were back upstairs in the room we had first entered. The waist-high windows looked across the fairway to the house where we had parked. The late afternoon sun was beaming at us, reflecting off a large window on the bank repo.

"Jesus, that's intense," Jimmy said. "Shut the fucking curtains."

I pulled the drawstring, and the curtains walked their way across the windows. That's when we saw Braxton's hiding place.

The curtains had broad hems in their bottoms. The sun lighted the curtains up from behind, and on the bottom of each one were several silhouettes of envelopes, slid into the hem.

We looked at each other and looked again at what a reflection of the desert sun was showing us.

"Gently," Jimmy said. He pulled a razor blade out of a small compartment on the golf bag.

It turned out we didn't need it. The ends of each hem were turned inward, holding the envelopes inside the hem. The first one dropped to the floor as I pulled it out. It was marked "Wave runner." Wave runner had four grand in it. "Mountain Bike" had six grand. "Fridge" had eight hundred bucks. It went on like that. It looked like the entire Craigslist inventory was in the envelopes in those curtains. We shoved them all into the bottom of the golf bag.

We went downstairs looking for more curtains to work on. There were none. We were back upstairs. No more curtains. It was time to leave.

That's when we heard it.

The front door opened. Voices.

"I don't give a good goddamn who you are or what fed-er-allies you jokers are from." It was Detective Glover. "You pay your way in here if you want a look-see. That Chicago guy dropped four hundred. You can do the same."

"We don't play those games." It was Agent Fitch. "You're blocking a federal investigation. You want to spend fifteen years in the slammer?"

"You want a load of double aught in your backside?" Glover asked. "Detective Duffy has your asses covered. It could be an accident here about to happen. Call me when you have four hundred. I'll have a car posted out front until you do."

We heard them walk out the front door. Outside Glover spoke again.

"You know, you boys maybe should let me check with your superiors to make sure you really are who you say you are."

"No need, we'll get you the four hundred," Fitch said. "Be back in an hour."

"Make it two hours," Glover said. "It's happy hour. Don't rush."

We looked around to make sure we hadn't left anything behind. I looked once more at the empty closet with the yellowing newspaper sitting on its shelf. Something made me grab it. Why the hell would anyone want an old paper, I thought. Was there a reason? I shoved it into the golf bag.

We went smoothly down the staircase and out into the fairway, where we started to resemble two guys playing twilight golf. Two minutes later, we were in the Caddy, pulling out of the driveway of the bank repo.

"You know Cassandra's been wanting a place like this," Jimmy said. "Big enough for parties, overlooking a nice golf course."

"Yeah, too bad about the lousy security," I said.

"Yeah, too bad." Jimmy laughed.

The Caddy purred as we drove away.

CHAPTER THIRTEEN

We drove back to Ribs by Gus.

Gus looked up from the counter as we entered with the golf bag in tow.

"Use the office," he said. "I'll bring you some beers."

In minutes we had the contents of the golf bag's side pouch all over the desk. There were 23 envelopes. All had cash, and all were labeled. A quick look at the craigslist listings on the thumb drive I had from Braxton's computer matched the envelopes.

Jimmy counted the money three times.

"Forty-two thousand, eight hundred," he said. "More than I make an hour."

"Yeah, me too," I said. "This ain't Jacky's two million."

"No," Jimmy said. "It's Braxton's running money and he ain't running no more."

A knock on the door.

"It's Gus with the beers," Gus said.

Jimmy got up and opened the door.

"We're figuring it out, Gus. Take a few more minutes."

Gus took a look at the mess on his desk and turned to leave.

"Take all night if you want," Gus said. He laughed and shut the door behind him.

"Like I said, good people," Jimmy said. "His family goes way back."

I sipped my beer. Something wasn't right about the labeled envelopes.

Jimmy beat me to it.

"He marks every envelope like it's some prize he's going to show to someone," Jimmy said. "Once when Cassandra was visiting her mother in New York, she talked me into selling her old Jaguar on Craigslist. Some goofy limy finally showed up and bought the lemon for eight grand, cash. I stuck it in one of those envelopes from Dominic's Sports Betting and labeled it 'Jaguar Paris Trip.' She got the hint. France was fun."

"You had a partner," I said. "You labeled the envelope so you could brag to her and give out a hint."

"Yeah," Jimmy said. "So, who's Braxton's partner? He wasn't married. You see anyone crying over him?"

"Marcy Feldstein says everyone at Galloping Dominos thought he was a shit," I said. "The only person he hung with was Jerry Feldstein. The two of them were drinking buddies in Chicago. They hung at a place called Mister Freddie's. Dawn got that from Muriel. When Muriel and Jacky bought the liquor business, she put her foot down – no Jerry and probably no Neal Braxton."

"That Muriel's sharp," Jimmy said. "If that's the same Mister Freddie's in Elmwood Park, Jerry and Neal might have been more than buddies. All male clientele and I don't mean a topless joint."

I took a deep drink from my beer.

"So, Braxton's saving the envelopes with the writing on them to show Jerry that he's sold their toys at a good price, and now they can run off together?" I asked.

"Yeah, Art Feldstein couldn't leave his loser son in Chicago working for Muriel and Jacky, so he brings him out to Vegas and ends up with Neal Braxton for a bonus."

"So, are you thinking Jerry popped Braxton so he could have it all? He didn't stick around to collect what we found."

"Hard to say," Jimmy said. "Maybe it was a jealous choir boy from Mister Freddie's."

"When Detective Duffy came to interview Marcy and Jerry about Braxton's shooting, Jerry ducked out to go play golf with some guy from Detroit."

"Is that the same Duffy that held a shotgun on Fitch, and what's his name?"

"Yeah, Fitch and Rice."

"They're desperate to find something," Jimmy said. "They might be feds, but they ain't kosher."

"We got a strange cast of characters here," I said. "Duffy and Glover are playing small ball. A couple hundred here, four hundred there, it's your typical cop on the take, big shot at the bar act. I don't think Fitch and Rice are in it for small dough. They want Charlemagne or his manager for what they know or maybe for what they have."

Jimmy leaned forward and looked at the mess of envelopes.

"The redneck that got squished, the Russians you told me about?" He asked. "They're after the magician and his manager for the same thing, yeah?"

I nodded.

"There's something you got to see," I said. "Turn out the lights."

In the pitch-black, I placed four of the Aramaic coins on the desk. A light blue glow came from one coin, then another. Soon all four coins were glowing a bright blue.

"Jesus," Jimmy said. "These things ain't gonna blow up, are they?"

"Far as I can tell, they're okay," I said. "It's part of what some of our players are after. They're looking for Charlemagne or Old Zeke, figuring they have it."

As your eyes adjusted, it was possible to see parts of the room. Jimmy's face had a blue glow about it. He touched one of the coins.

"It hums," he said.

He moved the coin about a foot from the other three. When he let go, the coin slid back to the other three. He pushed the coin again about a foot, but this time he kept his finger on it. The other three coins slid over to where he held the coin.

"I found some of these in the theatre after Charlemagne boogied," I said. "The redneck Jeff Davis had four of these on him when they dragged him from under the bus. One of these was in a handful of coins that came off Braxton's body. I don't think Glover was aware of much at the time. He was just handing me some change after he had picked Braxton clean – first order of business at a homicide."

"The way these coins just moved," Jimmy said, "that's the way things moved in the Charlemagne show. Everything was bigger, but it had that way about it."

I looked down at the coins. Each was face up with the Ezekiel lettering showing. I turned one coin over to show the double pyramids that formed the Star of David. The other coins backed away. I turned over another coin. It came back to the lone coin.

I reached over and turned on the light. The blue glow disappeared. Jimmy shoved all the coins together, two up, two down. They sat there, inert.

"You put them in your pocket," Jimmy said. "It's dark in there. Don't they light up and move around?"

"No, that's why the other coins were in the sack when I found it. If the quarters or batting cage tokens are in between the Aramaic ones, nothing happens. One coin by itself doesn't light up."

Dealing with four coins on a desk was one thing; dealing with forty-two grand and change was another. We owed Gus for his cooperation. He knew we had been heading to Braxton's house. He saw us counting money. We had a desktop full of it. I had no idea how much was right for Gus. With some guys, it's an act, all linguini, and no sausage.

"Gus should get a taste," I said. "How heavy is he?"

Jimmy swallowed some beer.

"Club Diamond in McHenry," he said. "Gus's family owned the joint, gambling, and ladies for hire. They sold the biz for a good profit to the Tortoni Brothers out of Jersey, but Gus's dad kept the land and the building in his name. Word is they carried some paper on Ralphie Tortoni, the older brother."

Jimmy took a swig from his beer and continued.

"Ralphie had a white powder up the nose problem. This made it difficult to pay bills. He couldn't even handle the vig on the loan. Wouldn't you know it, Ralphie tried to ruin St. Patty's Day in Chicago when they found what was left of him floating in the bright green Chicago River."

"What happened then?" I asked.

"Tony Tortoni, the younger brother, hands the business back to Gus's dad. Dad gets Dickie Masino to reopen the place, over-order everything on Tony's credit, and fence everything out the back door. Next thing you know, there's a fire. The joint's a total loss, but the insurance pays off. About a year later, Gus's dad sells the land for twice its worth to the county for a mental health center. He had the county commission in his pocket."

"So, whatever happened to Tony Tortoni? He still around?"
"Whatever happened to Jimmy Hoffa?"
Jimmy shrugged.
"So, what do you say to ten grand for Gus?" I asked.
"Maybe a little generous," Jimmy said.
"We should be generous with Gus," I said.
"Yes, we should."
Jimmy nodded.

CHAPTER FOURTEEN

We made our way from Ribs by Gus to the lot where Jimmy's Caddy was parked. I carried the golf bag. Jimmy had two red food delivery bags. Each bag had sixteen thousand and change in it. Some tip, eh? Mine also had the yellowed newspaper from Braxton's closet – a mystery bonus.

The golf bag had six beat-up irons. A Springfield rifle with a scope was tucked in next to an over-sized driver. Both had leather sock covers.

"Hell of a rifle," I said. "Never noticed it was there."

"I keep it handy," Jimmy said. "Hemingway used it in Africa."

"And what, you borrowed it from him?"

"No, Jesus. Same model. It ain't his."

"Just checking," I said.

Gus waved to us as we drove out of the parking lot.

Jimmy's cell phone rang. He put Cassandra on speaker.

"We just left Gus's rib joint. I got Nick here with me, say 'Hello'."

"Hey Nick. I just came from Dominic's Sports Betting. The Hawks paid off at sixteen to one. I turned in our slips – one each for you guys and the two I bet."

"Babe, I'm delighted," Jimmy said. "Can we take Nick out for a drink?"

"I'm tied up with news and features, but I can meet you two at Rusty's around ten."

"Sounds about right," Jimmy said. I nodded my okay.

"Nick," Cassandra said. "I have a connection for you. Talk later."

We floated toward the strip in the purring Caddy.

Disappearing Act

"Jesus, it's been a day of hitting long shots," Jimmy said. "That Hawks thing paid nice, and the Braxton thing was wonderful."

I turned to him with my best Dirty Harry.

"You feeling lucky, Punk?"

"Shit, who wouldn't?" Jimmy said. "Before you came by, I had an eight-to-one-shot come home at Keenland."

"Let's try one more long shot. Maybe scare up another player in our game."

We cruised into Sunset Park with two pizzas. We had a couple cases of beer in cheap plastic coolers loaded with ice.

"Nothing like a ballgame under the lights," Jimmy said. "You think Old Zeke might show his face?"

"Just a hunch," I said. "He likes Karen enough to let her use his high-tech bat. He may be lurking somewhere at the Vegas Dykes game."

We unloaded our beer and pizza to the empty Dykes bench. The Dykes were in the field. According to the scoreboard, they had a six to nothing lead over the Witnesses.

"Catchy name," Jimmy said. "Must be a bunch that works at the courthouse."

"Maybe it's the witness protection program."

We both laughed.

I looked for Old Zeke in the stands. He wasn't there. A few cars and vans were parked beyond the outfield fences. Was he among the people who were watching the game from lawn chairs beside their vehicles? Grills were doing dogs and burgers.

The Witnesses batter popped up to the shortstop for the third out.

Karen spotted us as she came off the field.

"Hey, you showed up. Great."

"We brought pizza and brews," I said. "There's enough here for the team."

The response was immediate. The team was hungry and thirsty.

"Let's get a batter up here," the umpire said. He started to walk over.

"He's gonna give us shit for bringing pizza and beers," Jimmy said.

Disappearing Act

I should have bet Jimmy a sawbuck on that one.

"Hey, if you could spare a beer, I sure could wet my whistle," the umpire said.

"No problem," I said. The flow was going our way.

Or was it?

Walking behind the umpire were two Witnesses ballplayers. As they drew closer, the lettering on their shirts became clearer. These weren't any witnesses. These were God's Witnesses.

"We object to alcohol being served at a mixed league event."

She was wound tight. Her head wore a helmet of blond fiber that could have passed for hair had the hairspray been chiseled off. For a minute, I thought the horn-rimmed glasses were part of the wig assembly. If you popped everything from her head, you might find a real person underneath, freed from the Halloween headpiece.

"We've been down that road," the umpire said. "There's no rule banning beer."

She was silent. Her partner spoke.

"Well, this is supposed to be a mixed league. Where are the men on the team?"

He was the guy that everyone wanted to beat up in high school. His God's Witnesses shirt was heavily starched. A gold cross hung on a chain. It swung back and forth over the lettering "God's." His hair was real, but it was cut like a cheap toupee.

I looked at Jimmy.

"Are these the born-again morons that the Vegas Visitors Bureau keeps denying that they exist?" I asked.

"Sir," Starched Shirt said. "I forgive your insolence, but you have no standing here. Even our affirmative action umpire will tell you there are supposed to be some men on this team, and although some of these women resemble men, they are not men."

I wanted to hit him. His team was losing, and he was looking for a way out, an excuse. The Dykes were cheaters. The umpire was black. Alcohol was present.

Lawyer Cox had an answer.

"My good man," Jimmy said. "Both Nick and I have been recruited to be on this team. Karen has invited us, and should we measure up, we will with pride – gay pride, I'm sure you've heard of it- be happy to join the Dykes and play against your misguided team of Christians."

"You can't play. You don't have uniforms," Starched Shirt said.

"That's not a rule," the umpire said. "Dress is optional. Your team can play naked if they want. Nothing in the league rules."

The two Witnesses walked away.

Starched Shirt turned.

"I will certainly pray for you and your misguided ways tonight," he said.

"Right back at you, Pal," one of the Dykes yelled.

Karen penciled the two of us in as the eleventh and twelfth batters in her line up, which meant we didn't have to embarrass ourselves in the field. Still, we could sit on the bench and heckle Witnesses batters. Each male batter, we decided, got named "Judas." Each female batter became "Magdalene."

"Hey, here's Judas. The Lord is trusting him to get a hit."

"Magdalene's up. She's carrying a big stick for the Lord."

We finally got up in the fifth inning. I got a scratch hit past the shortstop. Jimmy walked. Our next hitter, Marlene, wasted no time hitting the first pitch over the centerfielder's head. It bounced off the fence, and I headed for home. As I rounded third base, I looked back at centerfield. Had I seen a large bearded man waving us on as the ball came to the fence? If I had, he was gone as I crossed the plate. Three of the vehicles beyond the centerfield were starting their engines and pulling away. Jimmy crossed the plate, followed by Marlene.

"Mercy rule," the umpire said. "Score's 13 zip. The Dykes have won."

The Game was over.

We tried to trade traditional high fives with the Witnesses, but they drove off, not wishing to touch the hands of unwashed lepers. We gave each other high fives and shared a few with Tim, the umpire, who turned out to be a decent guy.

We hung out for a while with the Dykes, finishing up the beer and the pizza. Marlene turned out to be an attorney who had practiced in Kankakee, Illinois. She remembered hearing about Jimmy and his "retirement" to Vegas.

Disappearing Act

"What could I do?" He asked. "They were both sniffing around for stock options and no-interest, no payback loans. I was caught between a large donkey and an enormous elephant. No way they were taking the fall. I wasn't going to either. I had them both on tape. The only thing the Democrats and the Republicans could agree on was this whole thing had to go away. So here I am, retired to Vegas."

"Yeah, I got tired of all the political bullshit, too," Marlene said. "Cindy and I packed the car one night and never looked back. I'm doing adoption services and some family law. At first, we lived on what she made cleaning teeth."

"We're all refugees," Tim the umpire said. "You come back from serving your country, and there's no work. Your medical care gets doled out like they've only got four aspirin and a bandage. I do valet parking and work part-time at FedEx. I'm trying to get a dealer job at Bellagio."

Karen came over and gave me a fake punch in the arm.

"You guys, you guys," she said. She shook her head.

"Yeah," I said. "I guess we sorta screwed up your game."

"Only in the best of ways," she said. "You two devils are just what we needed."

I gave her my card with my cell phone number on it. She gave me a Feel Da Dreams card with her number on it, plus a 50 percent discount on batting tokens. We'd stay in touch. I didn't know how long I'd be in town, but I might be available for another game or two if needed.

It was time to go.

Jimmy cruised the Caddy toward the outfield, where a few hangers-on were still roasting hotdogs and drinking beers. We stopped and got out to look where Old Zeke maybe had been standing near the centerfield fence. There were a few cigarette butts. I couldn't tell if they were French. No package on the ground. No coins glowing in the dark.

"Hey, Fellas," a voice behind me said. "You're the guys from the ballgame. I recognized your Cubs shirt."

He was a thin guy, maybe in his late eighties.

"I'm John," he said. "I come out to watch the games and swap tall tales with this bunch out here."

We shook hands. His grip was firm.

"I'm Nick," I said. "Visiting from Chicago. This is Jimmy. He's a reformed lawyer."

"I guess I've heard it all, now," John said.

We all laughed.

"Your friend, Old Zeke, was here rootin' you on. He said to tell you he'd be in touch. Says he may be needing your help."

"You see him here often?"

"He shows up now and then. Loves to tell stories about storms in the desert and how people need to have more respect for each other. Smokes those stinky French cigarettes, but tonight he brought some beers so I can't complain."

I handed John my card.

"If you see Zeke before we do, have him call," I said.

"You bet I will," he said.

We said our goodbyes and drove toward Rusty's.

CHAPTER FIFTEEN

The strip was lit up in all its glory as we drove to Rusty's to meet Cassandra.

"Nick, you're a crazy son of a bitch," Jimmy said. "Most guys come into town to collect, find the guy, lean on him to hock jewelry, sign over his car, and be on their way, but not you. You get a couple people killed, get a couple Russians involved, and have us join a lezzie ball team. Next thing I know, I'm involved in breaking and entering and paying off some third-generation goombah."

I watched him swing the Caddy across two lanes.

"Yeah," I said.

"It gets worse," he said. "Now you got me worried about phony government agents, some desert rat named Old Zeke, and who killed Neal Braxton, a guy I detest."

"Sorry, Jimmy," I said.

"Sorry, Hell. I'm having the time of my life."

Sinatra was singing, "The Best is Yet to Come," as we entered Rusty's. It was an upscale bar without being glitzy or trendy. The place was half-filled with couples at the bar and a crowd of seven or eight around a large table.

The barkeep, a guy who looked like he could have gone ten rounds with Jake La Motta, or for that matter could have been Jake La Motta, saw Jimmy and motioned toward a booth in the back. Cassandra sat, trying to hold back a laugh as we approached.

"You guys can't make up your minds whether you're delivering food or playing golf?" She pointed at the red food delivery bags and the golf bag.

"We've had a full day," Jimmy said, kissing her. He unzipped a delivery bag and slid her hand into it. She felt around. Her expression went from curious to happy as she peeked at the cash inside.

"Wow," she said. "We said we'd always have Paris. It looks like we might be having it again."

We laughed.

The waitress came. We ordered three Chicago style Italian beef sandwiches and a pitcher of beer.

We recounted our afternoon and evening for Cassandra.

She liked the part about sneaking across the golf course into the late Neal Braxton's house.

"That's absolutely crazy that they would have the front of the house secured and leave the back of it wide open," she said. "I know there's a shortage of patrol personnel, but there must be a shortage of brainpower, too."

We told her about Detective Glover trying to over-charge Fitch and Rice for admission into Braxton's house. His threatening to contact their superiors to see if they were really who they said they were got a laugh.

"That's priceless," Cassandra said. "I never knew Jake Glover had it in him."

Then we got to the part about joining the Las Vegas Dykes softball team.

"Whoa," she said. "Let me get this straight – no pun intended- you two are members of a lesbian softball team?"

"Well, we got to play tonight," Jimmy said. "We each scored a run, and we beat the hell out of God's Witnesses by a score of 13 zip. I almost had to pull Nick out of a fight with the Witnesses' manager, a real turd."

He gave her a few more details of our game and how the Dykes were "good people."

"Marlene, she's the one who hit the homer that let Nick and me score. She's a lawyer. Her partner Cindy cleans teeth. Used to live in Kankakee."

Cassandra turned to me and smiled.

"Living with Jimmy sometimes gets strange, Nick," she said. "He's full of crazy betting schemes. And he has me hanging around with some wild characters, but I love him, and I love how he's brainwashed me into his version of reality, but then you come to town. All of a sudden, the craziness gets stretched even more. Tell the truth, Nick. Does Dawn keep you on a leash when you're in Chicago?"

We laughed. Tears of laughter were coming from Cassandra.

Then she was serious, with tears still streaming.

"That ballgame is one of the most beautiful goddamn things you two have ever done," she said. "I'm so damn tired of moralist thugs trying to kick people around."

We finished the food.

"I have someone for you to talk to," Cassandra said. "She's working tonight, but she's available tomorrow morning. You could meet her for breakfast at your hotel in the coffee shop. She said nine would be fine. Her name is Doris."

"Hooker Doris?"

"None other than," Cassandra said.

I was back at my hotel at eleven. As I approached the door to my room, I saw the "Do Not Disturb" tag on the door handle and yellow streaks on the red hall carpet. I expected red streaks on the yellow rug inside my room. Someone had visited me.

Before leaving, I had squirted ketchup and mustard in streaks that blended into each colored rug.

A close look at the hall had my visitor heading for the staircase exit.

I entered my room and found red stains. The place had been searched. My clothes were where I had left them. Everything else was down in the car or in the safe at Cassandra's office.

I had the old newspaper from Braxton's closet with me. I had grabbed it on a hunch. Was there anything of value in it?

It didn't take long to find the feature on Ted Evans, who liked calling himself Old Zeke. According to the article, the former NASA astrophysicist was an admirer of acts like Penn & Teller, and Siegfried & Roy. He was now interested in bringing multimedia shows to Vegas. Evans was a fan of Pink Floyd and other groups using sophisticated electronics in their presentation. He was open to proposals.

The article mentioned Evans suing the government for wrongful dismissal over misuse of government patents and methods. The piece said Evans received what was believed to have been a seven-figure out-of-court settlement.

I was about to put the paper down when I realized it was two sections, each from a different date.

The second section had an article titled "Southern Political Group Convenes in Boulder City amid Minority Protests." Pictured with several friends was the late Jeff Davis of under the tour bus fame.

A spokesman for the Confederate Front, Ashley Beauregard, explained his group.

"We want to reinstate the grandeur of the Confederacy," he said. "Many people fail to see the beauty of what was destroyed by the Northern invasion of a sovereign country. Just as Viet Nam has once again risen from destruction from the same interventionist armies, the Confederate States of America will do likewise. We have the money and the people to oppose and resist the occupying army of the North. It's only a matter of time until we reclaim our sacred honor and values."

Demonstrators outside the Confederate Front meeting were quick to voice concerns about the group.

"These people are crazy and dangerous," said Willie Washburn, spokesman for the People's Common Alliance. "They're talking about shooting minorities on sight. We understand they are endorsing bombings of federal facilities and have even talked about raising a private army."

I noticed the dates on each newspaper. The one touting Evans, aka Old Zeke, was from a year and a half in the past. The paper talking about the Confederate Front was two months old.

I put the security lock on the door and washed out my Cubs shirt in the bathtub as I thought about the first article.

Maybe that was how Braxton got Charlemagne into the Galloping Dominos Casino. The Liberace impersonator wasn't pulling the numbers, so Braxton maybe got in touch with Evans to see what kind of a show he might be able to do.

The second newspaper article was a mystery. What did Braxton care about the Confederate Front? They were in this game all right. Jeff Davis died under a tour bus trying to grab the Aramaic coins.

I was too tired to think.

I hung my shirt to drip dry over the tub.

My email had a message from Dawn.

"I know you're busy. I hope things are going well. Molly and I miss you. Attached are two drawings from Molly. One is of you, the other is Seymour, the sun bear in his cage at the zoo. Stay safe, Babe."

The resemblance surprised me. Seymour and I could have been long lost brothers. I made a mental note to smuggle a hacksaw to Seymour when I got back to Chicago.

CHAPTER SIXTEEN

I was up and showered by seven. It gave me time to watch the early Vegas news.

If it bled, it led.

A fourteen-year-old girl shot two creeps trying to enter her house in Northwest Vegas. A convenience store robbery had both robber and clerk dead. A stabbing outside a downtown hotel had one critical at a local hospital. Meanwhile, police officials blamed the rise in crime to California's early release of prisoners doing time for drugs, and the shortage of patrol personnel to cruise city streets.

It sounded like Chicago, except the shooting wasn't confined to police and black teenagers. In Vegas, everyone was encouraged to get in on the act.

One sponsor of the early news was a gun store. Another was a bail bondsman. A pawnshop, a payday loan outfit, divorce lawyers, ambulance chasers, a detox place, and an escort service formed the rest of the advertising parade.

Next, the news reported on squatters taking over abandoned houses all over the county. Some were in high-priced neighborhoods, which now had crack houses on their blocks. The next report was a dramatic increase in syphilis in Vegas and Clark County.

It wasn't happy talk news. Vegas was the 21st-century version of the wild, wild west.

I looked around my room. I stepped over the ketchup and mustard stains on the rug and phoned the desk.

"I'm checking out and going over to the Luxor," I said. "If anyone wants me, I'll be in a deluxe tower premier suite. I'll settle up when I get downstairs."

Then I called the Bellagio and booked a room. Whoever had tracked mustard and ketchup around my place could do it at the Luxor. It was time to meet Hooker Doris for breakfast.

I had no idea what Hooker Doris looked like. I could have guessed busty blonde or motorcycle chick with tattoos or flamboyant redhead in tight capris. Was she a Vietnamese girl in a black dress or a black woman wearing a low-cut blouse? Maybe an English babe speaking with a hard-to-understand Cockney accent would have been one of the decent guesses, but all would have been wrong.

I scanned the restaurant. The place had retired couples and groups of conventioneers wearing nametags. I was about to leave, figuring I had been stood up when a voice came from one of the booths where I stood.

"Are you Nick?"

I turned. Someone was sitting in what I thought was an empty booth. She was small with red hair in braids and a freckled face. If she was five feet tall, it was stretching it.

"Are you Doris?" I asked.

"Yes," she said. "Cassandra said you'd buy me breakfast."

I slid in across the table from her and motioned for the waitress.

"I confess," I said. "I had no idea what you looked like. I guess I should have asked Cassandra last night."

"It's okay," She smiled. "I kinda like surprising people, but I figured it was you. Cassandra said you were Chicago, so your shirt and hat kinda gave it away."

She paused, then said, "Plus, it looks like you're carrying. What are you packing if I may ask?"

"Just a Glock," I said. "Old reliable."

"Mine's a small Ruger. One empty chamber, one blank, the rest are loads. I carry it in my purse. It's never very far from the action. I've only had to fire the blank a couple of times. It's so loud. It stops all the nasty stuff from going any further."

The waitress came, and we both ordered the High Roller Special, which consisted of steak, eggs, pancakes, potatoes, juice, and coffee.

I like to ease people into talking by giving before I get. It opens things up.

Disappearing Act

"I'm here trying to track down someone missing," I said. "You probably heard about the sudden shut down of the Charlemagne show. I'm looking for whoever took off with the money owed to the theater. So far, I've made a little headway, and I've been able to enjoy Vegas a little. Vegas is different from Chicago, but there's also a lot in common. I was playing softball last night at one of the parks. We had pizza and beers in the dugout. Hell, I had a great time."

"I bet you did," she said. "I see a lot of different people in my life. Most just want to be happy. I've been hooking for the last six years. I look like I'm fifteen, but I'm really twenty-six. A lot of my trade is people who want to be fifteen again, women and men, both. I'm the blank canvas they play on. I'm their first love, the slightly naughty girl they can talk into doing the dirty. I never use a swear word. All the men have thingies, and of course, all their thingies are bigger than my uncle's thingy, which I tell them I once looked at through a keyhole. The women all have beautiful boobies. I'm still hoping that mine will get as big as theirs."

"Sounds like you do a lot of acting," I said.

"Yeah, I can blush at will, too," she said. To prove it, she blushed.

"Now that's talent," I said. We both laughed.

"Amateur shrink, too," she said. "I get paid better than most shrinks. I'm not cheap – fifteen hundred per person. I don't advertise. I'm strictly word of mouth. The danger is I'm taking a lot of it home. I have to quit soon. I've saved the money, so that's not it. There's a part that keeps me coming back for the next throw of the dice."

"I know the feeling," I said. "I came out here to collect money, find a guy who skipped, but now, I'm thinking money is only part of what I'm looking for. If you handed me the money right now, I'd still be trying to solve a mystery."

"Does that bring us to Agents Fitch and Rice?" She asked.

Our orders arrived. We were both hungry.

"Take your time," I said. "Enjoy the food."

Her food was gone in five minutes. I had half my plate left.

"I get some of my clients from the casino operators," she said. "Like I said, it's word of mouth. To the right client, I'm something special. I'm probably nothing to your average conventioneer or gambler."

She sipped her coffee and continued.

"Fitch calls my cell phone and says he and his friend want to take me on a magic carpet ride. He's got a deluxe suite at New York, New York. He mentions the person who recommended me, and I say 'okay, it's three grand, I'll meet you there at ten.'"

"Threesomes are no problem?" I asked.

"Usually, they're fine," she said. "I could go Freudian about latent homosexuality or dominance, but it's just different strokes for different folks. I'm not there to do a psych evaluation. I want my customers to have a good time, and I want to get paid."

The waitress brought more coffee.

"I got to their suite and realized they were high," Doris said. "I figured it was coke. There's so much of it around, it must be in vending machines."

"What happened then?"

"They had me take off my clothes and kneel on this blue plastic square. It was about two feet square and maybe an inch thick. 'Okay,' I said, 'What's next?' That's when Fitch starts mumbling about spatial shifts and parallel energy bonds. He had a small control panel about the size of a cell phone. He pressed a button, and the square I was kneeling on started to rise. It got to about a foot off the floor, and then it began to get bigger under me. It was about three feet wide now, and maybe that long."

"You must have been shocked," I said.

"I was. It was humming. Then Rice grabbed the controls, and things got scary. The whole thing jerked forward. I held on. A corner of the magic carpet – that's what they were calling it- smashed into a mirror on the wall and cracked it. I held on as it rose up a few feet. It turned fast and smashed right into the flat-screen TV. Pieces of it fell to the floor. Fitch grabbed the controls from Rice and did something. I looked across the room toward the closed drapes. I saw myself hanging onto the magic carpet. It wasn't a reflection. It was another me."

"You mean like a hologram?"

"I thought so at first, but then I raised one hand to see if it would respond. It did with the same hand I raised, my left. I said something like, 'Is that me?' It spoke back to me, but it came out garbled. I was totally freaked."

"Then what happened?"

"Fitch and Rice thought it was hilarious. They couldn't stop laughing. Someone pressed another button or two, and the magic carpet shrank to the size of a pack of cigarettes, and I fell to the floor. The hologram thing disappeared. I got up from the floor and noticed they were drinking champagne to celebrate what they had done to me. They were pretty far out of it by then."

She sipped more coffee and looked around the restaurant.

"I wanted my money. I wanted to leave. I was bruised, and these two guys were on their backs laughing out of control. I grabbed the controller and what had become of the magic carpet and stuffed them in my bag next to my gun. They never looked up. I got my clothes on and left."

"Did you grab their wallets, too?"

"Yeah, I thought maybe they were good for the three thousand, and I'd find it there, but there wasn't much money. There were some IDs and some security entry cards, the kind you slide into something to get through a gate. There was a date on each of them, but they had expired a couple years ago."

"What did you do then," I asked.

"That's the great part of being connected, Nick. I went home, put my gun away, cleaned up, and explained my problem to a friend who works at the jail. I couldn't make the toys work like they had when I was flying around the room, but I had them, and I knew Fitch and Rice wanted them. I wanted my money."

"Is your friend named Roland, by any chance?"

"No, it's his secretary, Estelle. She called Roland. He sent a couple cops over to the hotel. They picked up Fitch and Rice on a disorderly charge and brought them to the jail. I was there waiting. 'Here's the deal,' Roland told them, 'the lady gets three grand and you get your toys back. You pay the damages to your room and an out-of-court fee and we'll be square, or I can get real heavy.'"

"So, they came back with…?"

"Four grand," she said. "I got three like I deserved. They got their toys and their wallets back. Roland and Estelle split the rest. I took her to lunch the next day. She's a wonderful person."

"One more question," I said. "Who recommended you to Fitch and Rice?"

"Neal Braxton. I partied with him and his lover, Jerry."

CHAPTER SEVENTEEN

We were back at Dominic's Sports Betting Parlor. Jimmy liked my report on Hooker Doris and her trysts with Fitch & Rice and Neal & Jerry.

"You don't suppose she does Penn & Teller and Siegfried & Roy, too?" he asked. "She could be the Ampersand Angel."

I was about to add Donnie & Marie when Jimmy cut me off.

"Look who just busted in, along with Moe, Curly, and Larry."

Sammy Di Carlo, owner of Black Like Me Records and Country Cussin' Records, barged into the crowded room. His brain trust stooges stood next to him.

Sammy looked like a small refrigerator wearing a cheap suit. Whoever had designed Sammy's costume had more buckles and zippers than they had taste.

"What's dis," Sammy said as he bulldozed up to where Jimmy and I had been enjoying coffee. "Dis da Chicahgah Club? How come youse guys ain't in jail?"

He sat down across from us and told his brain trust to take a walk, "But not too far, hah hah hah. Jimmy here might be tryin' to get me on a wire, hah hah hah."

The Three Stooges stood over by the monitors showing the latest race from Florida, a mudder's delight being run in a tropical downpour.

"I'm out here visiting my daughter," Sammy said. "She says you're looking for the magician. Good luck with that. I saw that show. The broads were easy to look at, but that Charlemagne guy, Jesus, what a fag."

"I guess you heard that Neal Braxton got whacked," Jimmy said.

"Yeah, day after I got here," Sammy said. "I thought he was a little faggy, too. Don't matter much, though. Marcy runs the show over there. I don't know what Jerry does. I guess he keeps the customers happy."

I could have told Sammy that Jerry had been keeping Neal happy, but that was as they say, "too much information."

"I bet you're hopin' that faggy magician hasn't spent all the dough by the time you catch up to him," Sammy said. "You got any idea where he went?"

"Jacky's got a guy looking near Denver," I said.

"You got anything worth betting on?" Jimmy asked.

"No, just makin' the rounds," Sammy said. "Always lookin' for the next Elvis."

"There's an Elton John impersonator out at the Blue Baron Bar," Jimmy said. "He'd be delighted to meet you."

"Hah hah," Sammy said. "Let's go, boys. We got people to see."

Sammy and the Stooges rumbled off toward the door leading to the strip.

"Think we should have told him we joined the Vegas Dykes?" Jimmy asked.

"No," I said. "I don't think he likes baseball."

"You don't suppose Sammy's hunting for that cash, do you?" Jimmy asked.

"With any luck, he'll head for Denver," I said.

It must have been visiting day at Dominic's. I looked up from my cold coffee to see agents Fitch and Rice standing there in all their black-suited glory.

"Did we see you leaving the Neal Braxton residence the other night after meeting Detective Jake Glover?" Fitch asked.

"Do you know you've got mustard on the tip of your shoe?" I asked. "You boys got a part-time gig at Subway?"

"We're involved in determining Neal Braxton's cause of death," Rice said.

"Offhand, I'd say instant lead poisoning," I said. "Three slugs and no Neal. Did you boys need some help with that?"

"We think you might have bribed your way into Braxton's house that night," Rice said. "That's a second-degree felony."

"Third-degree felony," Jimmy said.

Who's this?" Rice asked. "Some kind of legal hotshot?"

"He's my spiritual advisor," I said. "He keeps me on the straight and narrow. He says there's no need to go around paying for it. I'm charming enough to get what I want for free. You'd be surprised how many hookers offer me money to play with their toys."

"Listen, wise guy," Rice said. "This is serious stuff. Nasty people are looking for the magician and his crowd. Foreigners, could be terrorists, and somehow Braxton was involved. Whoever got him won't stop there."

I looked at Jimmy. Jimmy looked at me. Together we did the non-committal shrug.

"Wise guys," Rice said. He and Fitch turned and walked toward the exit to the strip.

It was quick.

Two men wearing bright aloha shirts, cowboy hats, and sunglasses stepped in front of Fitch and Rice. They pulled pistols and fired. Gunshots echoed through Dominic's. Patrons ducked for cover. The two assailants ran toward the strip. Fitch and Rice crumpled to the floor.

I got to Fitch first. I held his head up. He was fading fast. I searched him for anything that might solve the mystery. He had a wallet and an electronic room key from the Excalibur. I left his gun alone and grabbed his card case and iPhone

"Ambulance," Jimmy yelled as he searched Rice. "Nine one one. Get the cops."

I looked at Jimmy. Sirens were approaching, and a crowd gathered around the two fallen agents.

"We gotta direct them in," I yelled. "These men need help."

We were out the door in seconds, standing on the strip. The ambulance pulled up.

"Some kind of shooting in there," I told the EMT.

A cop pulled up, flashing lights on.

"Been a shooting in there, officer," I said. "Someone arguing about money."

The cop and his partner headed into Dominic's.

Jimmy and I headed for his Caddy.

"I got the keys to their rental," Jimmy said. "Chrysler 200, grey. It's bound to be here in the lot."

It didn't take long to find the car. The trunk had been pried open, and the driver's side door window had been smashed. The vehicle had been ransacked. The upholstery had been slashed along with the headliner.

"Lousy detailing job," Jimmy said. "Didn't even hang the air freshener."

Jimmy drove toward the Excalibur while I sorted out what was left of Fitch and Rice – two wallets, two card cases, two iPhones, and the passkey for their room.

"Someone with crayons must have made these drivers licenses," I said. "They've each got a couple hundred in cash, a phony looking government ID and a couple iPhones that won't unlock without a six-digit code."

Time, as they say, was of the essence. We parked at Excalibur and hit the elevator for the Fitch and Rice floor. The hallway was quiet. I put my ear to the door of the suite and listened for any activity. Nothing. I backed away and knocked on the door with the butt of my gun. Nothing.

Jimmy slid the passkey into the slot, and we were in. A laptop sat on the desk. In the drawer were two items that looked like what Hooker Doris had described to me – the magic carpet and its controller. The next drawer down held several stacks of hundred-dollar bills banded like they had just come from the bank. Next to them were two boxes of Magnum loads.

Jimmy checked the closet. In the jacket of one suit was a plastic bag containing Ezekiel coins separated by quarters. In another pocket was a plastic bag with a couple ounces of cocaine in it.

I looked at the floor. Under the desk was a business card. I picked it up. It was the same card from the desert whorehouse that Boris and Alexi had given me with their phone number on it.

There was a knock on the door.

We both froze. I had hoped that the cops hadn't traced Fitch and Rice to the Excalibur. It seemed way too soon for that.

Another knock.

"Hey, y'all in there? It's Ashley. We're a bit early."

We waited in silence.

"We're about a half-hour early, Boss," another voice drawled.

"More like about forty minutes, anyhow," still another voice said.

"Catch us an elevator, Junior," Ashley said. "We'll sit down in the lounge and enjoy us some sour mash whiskey."

The elevator bell rang. We listened for their fading voices as they got on.

We gathered what we had found and tossed it into a "Welcome to Las Vegas" shopping bag. We were out the door and down the stairs to the parking lot. We stashed our bag in the Caddy and found our way to the main lobby. A sign pointed the way to the Parlay Bar.

Ashley Beauregard of the Confederate Front sat between the two men at the bar. Beauregard wore an unremarkable white golf shirt and brown slacks. His bookends wore the same remarkable outfits the assailants at Dominic's had worn, the garish aloha shirts, cowboy hats, and sunglasses.

I looked at Jimmy. He looked at me.

We moved to the far end of the bar and sat.

"So, someone dressed like that knocks off Fitch and Rice, and then they go have drinks downstairs from where Fitch and Rice are staying?" Jimmy whispered. "They're either stupid as shit, or someone's been set up."

"Hell, you heard them upstairs trying to meet with Fitch and Rice," I said. "You don't think there's something in the water in Mississippi, do you?"

"Yeah, the bodies of dead black people," Jimmy said.

We each ordered a beer.

"Let's watch what happens," I said. "If it's a set-up, it'll go down soon."

We watched the trio at the far end of the bar down their sour mash and order another.

A man wearing an Excalibur vest approached us.

"You gents have each been selected to receive five hundred dollars-worth of chips from our casino," he said. "Please follow me to the desk so I can give you them."

We followed him out the door as five plain-clothes cops went into the Parlay. In seconds, they were out with the handcuffed Ashley and his two good ole boys.

The Excalibur Vest explained we had been in danger in the Parlay. He had told the story about the free chips to get us out of the possible line of fire.

"Yeah, never mind that," Jimmy said. "You promised us each five hundred bucks in chips. Plus, we left our beers in there."

Bitching does get you somewhere, at least at the Excalibur. We got our five-hundred-dollar chips from the Vest and another round of beers from a bartender who was happy to tell us, "those red necks looked shaky to me the minute they walked in."

CHAPTER EIGHTEEN

Hanging at Excalibur increased the danger of getting caught in the Vegas justice system, an iffy bet at best. I began to realize Vegas was unique only in its excesses. Vegas was a prophecy telling the rest of the nation what it was becoming. Connection trumped legality.

We drove out of Excalibur in Jimmy's Caddy.

His cell phone buzzed. Cassandra was on speaker.

"You guys were at Dominic's? You okay?"

"Yeah, we saw it all go down," Jimmy said.

"TV says two guys wearing Hawaiian shirts started shooting? Who'd they shoot?"

"Fitch and Rice," Jimmy said. "We got to them and searched for what we could. Followed up with a visit to their place at Excalibur. Found some interesting stuff. The Confederate Front showed up, two of them dressed like the shooters at Dominic's. We saw the three of them get arrested in the Parlay Bar. Looked like a set up deal."

"The shooters were in the bar at Excalibur?"

"They looked like the shooters, but we don't think it was them," Jimmy said. "You'd have to be pretty dumb to shoot someone and then go hang out in the building where they live."

"Sounds like someone's cheating at chess," Cassandra said. "You didn't get hurt, did you?"

"No, we hit the floor when the shooting started. It was over in seconds."

"Nick okay?" She asked.

"Nick's okay," I shouted.

"Roland says they're going to run their prints for an ID," she said. "They were each carrying Smith & Wesson .357 Magnums. Nothing else on them, you guys are fast."

Disappearing Act

"We should meet later," Jimmy said. "Last night's Rusty's arrangement would be good."

I nodded.

"Same time, same place, Guys. Jesus, be safe."

We drove south on the strip, heading past the "Welcome to Las Vegas" sign. We needed time to think.

I counted four dead in the search for whatever the Charlemagne opus had in its clutches. Jeff Davis died under a tour bus, trying to grab the mysterious Ezekiel coins. Neal Braxton was gunned down in front of his home while trying to sell his toys and flee town. Now agents Fitch and Rice were on a slab after being gunned down at Dominic's. Three of the Confederate Front were in jail suspected of shooting Fitch and Rice.

Someone was playing heavy. Was it our Russian friends? Did Jerry Feldstein have a role in this? Or had another party dealt themselves in?

My cell phone rang.

"Is this Nick from last night at the ballpark?"

"Yeah, this John?"

"Yeah. I talked with you after the game. If you ain't doing something more important, Old Zeke would like to buy you a beer. Bring your friend Jimmy along. We're at the Busted Flush Dive Bar."

We made a quick U turn.

"We can be there in about ten minutes," I said.

The Busted Flush went back to the forties. Mention a name from the old days and there was a story about them drinking at the Busted Flush. Did Sinatra or Bugsy Siegel ever hang out there? Their pictures were hanging on the wall. Wouldn't that be proof enough in Vegas?

John sat across from Old Zeke in a booth at the far end of the bar. Old Zeke looked up as we approached.

"I'm glad you guys are here," he said. "I need some help. People are dropping like flies."

We sat down. John raised his hand. The barkeep brought over a pitcher of beer and four mugs.

"I know you're after the two million bucks that Braxton stole from Jacky," Old Zeke said. "Maybe I can help you find it. I've got troubles maybe you can help."

I nodded.

Jimmy nodded and sipped his beer.

"I used to work for NASA," Old Zeke said. "I was there to investigate anomalies in quantum mechanics. It started as theory. Was there any possible way that parallel realities from another dimension would have any impact on what we would experience as our crafts approached the speed of light?"

"Parallel realities?" Jimmy asked. "A little help, please."

Old Zeke laughed.

"Science Speak. I'm guilty. I'm surprised anybody understands anybody."

"I used to do the same thing with Legal Speak," Jimmy said. "I started to see it other places. Gambler Speak is another one."

"You a hunch player?" Zeke asked.

"At times," Jimmy said. "Usually, I get a strong picture of my horse coming home. I haven't had the Bears winning the Super Bowl image in a long time."

Old Zeke laughed and sipped some beer.

"The parallel realities theory would support your horse coming home if not in this reality, but in one of a multitude of realities," Old Zeke said. "In some of those realities, your horse would break its leg, or stop halfway through the race to take a crap, or maybe even someone shoots the jockey. Your quest in this situation would be to make sure you're tuned into the right reality."

"Never mind his horse," I said. "We're sitting here in the Busted Flush. You mean there might be other versions of the four of us sitting in other Busted Flush bars?"

"Yeah, according to the theory, it's all possible and it's all going on as we speak," Old Zeke said. "But that's all hard to prove. We don't have the talent to step into another dimension to see if Jimmy's horse stopped to take a leak."

Jimmy slugged some beer.

"So, it's all a wash," he said. "If we can't do it, it doesn't mean anything. It's just interesting to talk about."

"Yeah," Old Zeke said. "Until somebody accidents their way into our reality and leaves a few souvenirs behind. Ever hear of Roswell?"

"New Mexico," I said. "Flying saucers crashed. Story goes they recovered bodies of aliens and what was left of their crafts. I always thought it was a good story, one of those Twilight Zone things. They even had a show on TV for a while claiming that some of the people in Roswell were aliens. It was fiction, sort of a soap opera."

"Yeah, I always thought it was a good story, too," Zeke said. "I was all into the theory business at NASA. In that racket, as long as you stay theoretical and formulaic you can collect from Uncle Sam for a lifetime. They'll feature you at seminars, feed you well, let you travel all over meeting your counterparts in London and Moscow."

"Something changed you?" I asked.

He took a swig from his beer and looked around the bar.

"I had theoretical proof that alternate realities could be tapped into on a split-second duration, say one tenth of a second. It's like that flash where someone thinks they've seen a ghost or an animal that isn't there. It wasn't very sexy. We used high energy colliders and electron cameras and if we got a shot of a molecular gas that wasn't supposed to be where we were aiming, it was considered worthy of the next funding cycle, of course tying it to national defense."

Zeke sipped his beer and went on.

"There was always a desire for more powerful equipment. The theory was basically if we had the power, we could breach the barrier between what we had and what we might see from our brave new world of physics. Little did we know that the barrier had been breached for short periods during the late forties when the American Southwest became a testing ground for atomic weapons."

I looked at Zeke and decided to jump in.

"So, you're saying that some of the tests opened a window into another reality?"

He sipped his beer and looked around the bar as if he was making sure it was safe to talk.

"There were Roswell incidents," he said. "I'm not saying that any of them were at Roswell. That's what they were referred to. Artifacts were recovered that related to spatial shift and time warping. I had no idea the artifacts existed until I ran into Fitch and Rice, or whoever they are."

Disappearing Act

Jimmy was about to speak, but I caught his eye, shaking my head "no." I wanted Zeke to go on without any mention of what we knew of Fitch and Rice and their sudden demise.

Zeke looked at me. I nodded for him to go on.

"I had an idea how to come up with some rudimentary devices that would get us close to bridging the gap to another reality. I went so far as to apply for patents in the name of the government for the coins, the Ezekiel Coins. That's when the shit hit the fan."

"What happened?" Jimmy asked.

"I was out of line, according to my superiors. I was endangering national security, plus there were fallacies in my theories that wouldn't work and wouldn't be safe if I tried them. I can't say I was shocked, but I was pissed. I decided to rock the boat just so much."

"Just so much?" I asked.

"You know, not enough to get shot over it, but enough to make them want to pay me to go away. They dropped a bundle on me and put out a press release that I had settled a patent problem with the government over a method I had created, and I was now out on my own. They thanked me for my cooperation, and I took the money and ran."

I looked around the Busted Flush as Zeke continued his story. You could get lost in all the TVs blasting out sports and news. This wasn't the Busted Flush that Sinatra and Bugsy Siegel hung out in, if they ever had.

Zeke tilted his cowboy hat and wiped the sweat from his forehead with a blue cowboy scarf.

"I was a free bird with a generous settlement from Uncle Sam," Zeke said. "During my travels for NASA, I saw a lot of elaborate rock shows. Pink Floyd was my favorite. I knew I could engineer a spectacular show."

"So, you came to Vegas and announced you were available," I said.

"Yeah, and for a while nothing happened. It was only a week or so, but it seemed like forever. Finally, I got a call from Fitch and Rice. They wanted to partner on a show with a lot of special effects. I wondered what I needed them for. I know lasers, projectors, lighting, audio systems. What were they going to offer?"

"They brought their toys," I said.

Zeke took a swig from his beer.

"Yeah, they had the toys, but they weren't good at operating them. At first, they handed me some BS about the toys being from a workshop in Silicon Valley that did work for Disney. The more I worked with the toys, the more I realized these were way beyond NASA cutting edge."

John motioned to the barkeep for another pitcher.

"Bring some pretzels, too. Man can't live on beer alone."

"Anyway," Zeke said, "I finally got them to admit that these were Area 51 pieces from a Roswell incident. When it rains in the desert, we get flash floods. The security people at the government facilities are always replacing fences where a sudden rush of water causes a breach. Fitch and Rice brought the equipment out through one of the breaches. Don't know if they killed anyone in the process."

"You didn't try to back out?" Jimmy asked. "You were in dangerous legal territory."

"Yeah, I was scared, but the more I worked with the equipment, the harder it was to let go. It was a Faustian deal with two devils. I wanted to do a spectacular show. This one would blow everyone's mind. I went to see all the magic shows in town, and they were all great, but mine would be way better. I had toys from another dimension."

"You weren't worried that the Feds would bust you?" I asked.

"I held my breath for several months while I worked on readying the show. It seemed that no one was looking for the equipment. Once the show debuted, I figured we were fine. We'd be just another major Vegas attraction that brought money in like it was a gold mine. We were strictly an entertainment, nothing dangerous. I made a deal with Fitch and Rice that I would have control of the equipment and they would get a generous cut from the show each month."

"How generous?" Jimmy asked.

"They each got a hundred thousand each month. For that, they did nothing. The rest got taken out in rent for the theatre and a few extra expenses here and there."

"You mean Charlemagne and the rest of the cast, right?" I asked.

"There is no Charlemagne," Zeke said. "I hired some models for sessions at my place in the desert. I made working models of several composites. Three or four models would go into producing one cast member. We ended up with six altogether, Charlemagne and his five very sexy lady friends."

"They were like holograms?" I asked

"More like robots or golems, if you will," Zeke said.

I poured some beer into my mug.

"So, there were no humans in your show. It was all golems?"

"Yeah, the images of the humans were the skins of the golems," Zeke said. "There was a chance if you made a direct copy from a human to a golem something might happen. The human could get lost somewhere out there in the ether, so to speak. With golems, it didn't matter much. They were easily reformulated."

"Did you lose any people or golems?" I asked. I thought of Hooker Doris hovering on a magic carpet, confronting her golem.

"In the early stages a couple golems. Never in a show. By the time we premiered, everything was down tight. The equipment was in place. It was a sophisticated system. I could sit backstage and run the whole thing from my iPhone. I had cameras on the audience so I would have Charlemagne say hello to celebrities and wink at cute women. I'd even have Charlemagne plugging different eateries and watering holes. He'd say the cast was heading there right after the show."

"So, if everything worked, what went south?" Jimmy asked.

"Did you ever think you could make somebody mad at you by handing them a hundred thousand dollars each month?" Zeke asked. "That's how it started to get with Fitch and Rice. 'There must be more money in this,' they'd say. Then it started to be, 'other people would pay for this kind of technology. There could be millions or even billions,' they'd say."

"And who has that kind of money?" Jimmy asked.

"Foreign governments, terrorist groups." Zeke sipped some beer.

"The Russians, Alexi and Boris?" I asked.

"You mean Moscow World Circus, Bolshoi Global Circus, Moscow Global Circus United States Tour, Bolshoi World Circus European Tour, and God knows what other shows they've come up with?" Zeke laughed.

He sipped from his beer.

"Boris and Alexi are two of the sharpest showmen around. They've managed to thrive despite Andropov, Gorbachev, Yeltsin, and Putin. Their shows are spectacular. I've known them for about twenty years. I'd go to Moscow for my NASA duties and end up at one of their shows. They'd get the best talent and the best special effects and put together spectacular four-hour shows. Their interest in the Charlemagne equipment would be for making one of their elephants float around the main tent while nearly naked acrobats would dance on top of it."

"Boris and Alexi are looking for you." I said. "You trying to avoid them?"

"I don't want them involved in something dangerous," Zeke said. "I've been laying low ever since the show closed. I caught wind that Fitch and Rice were trying to shop the technology to someone with real money."

"The Confederate Front?" I asked. "I didn't know they were that heavy."

"They weren't going to pay for it, they were just going to take it and probably kill me in the process. There's a heavier player in the game. Ever hear of Colonel Jae Joo Kim?"

"Sounds Korean," Jimmy said. "North or South?"

"Kim's in it for himself," Zeke said. "He deals with whoever's the highest bidder. Could be ISIS, Viet Nam, North Korea, Pakistan, or Iran. He made his fortune betting against our housing bubble, big time. He plays dirty, drug smuggling, weapon shipments. I'm thinking he's behind Neal Braxton getting shot. He might have been the one that put that Confederate Front guy under that tour bus, too."

Jimmy gave me a look. I shook my head "no." It wasn't time to come clean. Zeke had a few holes in his act that needed filling. When we walked in, Zeke mentioned, "people are dropping

Disappearing Act

like flies." He had no way of knowing that Fitch and Rice had been killed. There were no IDs left on either man. Unless he had put the dime on them, Fitch and Rice were still alive in his book. Did Zeke try to get out from under by whacking Fitch and Rice and putting the blame on three rednecks?

I leaned forward, putting my face a foot from Zeke's.

"I'm here to collect two million bucks in rent, which you say you don't have. I don't quite buy that. You made plenty off the Charlemagne show. Now, if you say you gave the rent to Braxton and he stole it, that's one thing. We can work that out, but if you're bullshitting me, you've got more troubles than Colonel Kim trying to take your toys."

Zeke leaned back. He reached into his blue *Gauloises* pack and lit a cigarette.

"I'm trying to be straight with you guys. It's dangerous out there. People involved in this are dropping like flies."

"Name some of them," I said, "I'll give you Braxton and the redneck under the bus. Hell, in Vegas, that's old news. Who else?"

"It was on the news just before you came in," Zeke said. "Braxton's boyfriend Jerry and his dad, Art Feldstein were killed in a car bombing this morning at the Galloping Dominos. Jerry was the one who collected the rent the last two months."

As if on cue, the Busted Flush TVs came on with the local news. The car bombing at the Galloping Dominos that killed Jerry Feldstein and his dad Art led the way. The shooting of our two unidentified pals Fitch and Rice by two men wearing Aloha shirts and cowboy hats at Dominic's was next. Police had three suspects in custody in that case. The video feeds for both stories featured police tape and flashing lights on cop cruisers that could have fit any police story.

With only a sketchy report from each killing, the news mavens soon switched to a story about a teenager on the SlotZilla zip line ride who pissed on the crowd of gamblers at the Fremont Experience as he rode above them. Several of the interviewed victims said they thought it was raining. Others didn't notice.

That was followed by a story about the large outbreak of scorpions in the county. People were getting stung while walking their dogs at night. The news had a lot of video on scorpions. People kvetching about scorpions was next. According to one guy, it was the start of a Biblical plague on Vegas. He issued his prophecy while wearing a t-shirt advertising a desert whorehouse.

The news gave me time to think. Four more people were dead and three were in jail. Whoever was doing the killing wasn't shy about car bombing and shooting up a crowded bookie joint on the strip.

I had to get it together fast. Zeke was target number one with a bulls' eye on his chest. The toys could get him killed. If Colonel Kim was running the hunt for Zeke, the problem might be above my pay grade. If it was the Confederate Front hunting Zeke, it was probably below my IQ level.

I told myself to start slow and be thorough. Even though it might be time to panic, it was no time to panic.

"So, Zeke, you saw the report on the car bombing, and it spooked you?" I asked.

"Yeah, I gave Jerry the money, meant for Jacky in Chicago. You say Jacky never got it, and I believe it. Jerry was tight with Neal Braxton. Now they're both dead, and I'm sitting across from you. Are you here to collect or kill?"

"Hey, you invited us," I said. "If this was a mob hit, you'd be dead by now. No shooter would stick around having beers with you. Things don't work that way."

He looked around the Busted Flush. Sweat poured off his face. The cell phone in my pocket buzzed, but it was no time to break off to answer anyone.

"Yeah, I called you here because I didn't know what else to do," Zeke said. "I thought you guys were great with Karen and the Vegas Dykes. I also have a lot of respect for Cassandra Black. She interviewed me several times for the show. I know she's close to both you guys."

"That's true," I said. "But what's your plan? You just going to hang around dodging rednecks, Colonel Kim, and your friendly Russians until one of them kills you?"

Zeke lit a cigarette and leaned back.

John poured beer into the mugs on the table.

"Zeke's way too decent for this shit," he said

"I feel like running," Zeke said. "The Confederates and Colonel Kim are after the toys. If either gets hold of them, they won't be toys for long. It's like opening a Pandora's box. They'll be weapons. When Fitch and Rice started marketing the toys, they brought Colonel Kim and the Confederate Front people to see the show on different nights. I don't know how many potential buyers they had on their list. I just know they wanted me to be done with the toys in three months. They told Braxton and Jerry that the show would end then. I decided to cut it by a month. I played along with Fitch and Rice. Yeah, everything was fine. We had our run. I had enough money."

"You didn't think to call Jacky for some help?" I asked.

"I was only a tenant in the theater. For all I knew, Jacky was in on the deal to sell the toys. Chicago has, well, you know not the best reputation in the world."

I looked around the room to see if anyone was paying extra attention to us. They weren't. They were busy being Vegas.

"So, you managed to close the show a month early, fooling everyone?"

"Yeah," Zeke said. "I had all the lighting and sound equipment ready to go into cases along with the toys. I stayed half the night and had it packed for the van. John helped, and by three in the morning, we were out at my place, unloading it into a heavy-duty storage container."

I sipped my beer, ignoring the buzzing iPhone in my pocket. I looked at Jimmy. He grimaced back at me. I plunged on.

"So, with your toys, you can float golems through the air, make things they're riding in change size and shape, change colors of things and make your golems and their equipment appear and disappear? You do this in an enclosed theater. Does this work out in the open, like smuggling a spy across a border or bringing something like anthrax over a border?"

"It could," Zeke said. "What we have now would do some of that, but you'd have to be pretty close to the action to get anything to happen, like maybe three hundred yards over a border. I was told there was another piece that boosted the toys. It's something they were calling the Magic Carpet. If you put it together with my toys, you could take down fighter planes, create plagues, do remote control terrorism. There'd be no end to the damage."

"Magic Carpet?" I asked.

"It was all possible, according to Fitch and Rice. They said one was stored in Area 51. By itself, it's a fancy toy that does some of what my toys do. If you hook it in with my stuff, it gets real strong, real fast, but they never got their hands on one, and I don't think they want to go back to get it."

I didn't want Zeke to know that Fitch and Rice were never going back for anything or that we had the Magic Carpet. I had another question.

"So, you've got your toys in a storage container out on your property. You've also got some people gunning for you, the types that shot Braxton and blew up the car today, taking Jerry and dear old Art out of the picture. How do you plan to deal with that?"

He looked around again and lit another cigarette.

"It's the worst situation," he said. "You can't call the government and tell them you have some of their toys from Area 51. Come and get them. The Feds say none of that exists. You're another cuckoo. So, if you can't turn them back in, do you run away with them? Hide them? Destroy them? Meantime if Fitch and Rice find where my place is, they could easily bring Colonel Kim out, and I'd be sitting there dead."

I looked at him. He was a man who had bought into a dream and ended up in a nightmare. If he held onto his toys, he was a target. If he got rid of his toys by handing them to the rednecks or Colonel Kim, they'd probably kill him anyway.

"You say Fitch and Rice could bring this Kim character out to your place?" I asked. "Have any of them been there before?"

"No, I saw Kim once at our show through Charlemagne's eyes, but he's never been out there. Fitch and Rice have a pretty good idea of the area I live in."

"Anybody else in this fiasco? I know John's been out there. Who else?"

Zeke sipped his beer and thought for a minute.

"The models that we made the composites out of for the golems, but that was over a year ago, and they never knew what we were doing it for. I told them it was for a Silicon Valley action game. Most people have a hard time finding the place. I had to shuttle the models in from town. The FedEx guy knows where I am, but that's about it."

"What else can you tell me about this Colonel Kim?" I asked. "Think hard. Did Fitch and Rice say anything about meeting him at a hotel? Any idea where he stays when he's here?"

"He owns one of those apartments in the Veer Tower over at City Center," Zeke said. "I hear he has a couple of bodyguards built like big torpedoes. He's got a girlfriend, a black singer named Pipes. He's been pushing her career in lounges around town."

"Here's something you can do for both of us," I said. "Take John and head for your place in the desert. Fitch and Rice are tied up with the police for now. They're persons of interest in that bookie joint shooting."

"They were involved in that?" Zeke asked.

"They may be on ice for a while," I said. "I have your cell number. I want you to be safe while Jimmy and I see what we can do about your dilemma. There's still a chance we can scare up that two million bucks, and maybe we can do something about Kim."

He looked at both of us for a minute and nodded.

"Jesus," he said. "I hope to Hell you can."

"Damn straight." John nodded.

They slid out of the booth and hurried out the door.

CHAPTER NINETEEN

We got to the street and saw Zeke and John take off in a white van. Jimmy steered his Caddy for Cassandra's office. We each had cell phone messages from Dawn, Jacky, and Cassandra. I also had calls from Vegas Dykes Karen and Hooker Doris.

At Cassandra's newspaper, the conference room was quiet and had a speakerphone in the center of a large table. It also had fresh coffee and a tray of bagels with all the trimmings.

Cassandra had already talked with Jacky and Dawn, letting them know that Jimmy and I had survived the Dominic's shooting, which was getting big play on CNN.

"Mobster Hit at Vegas Bookie Joint!"

That story soon took a back seat on the same network.

"Car Bombing at Vegas Casino Kills Former Chicago Booze Baron!"

Cassandra also told Jacky and Dawn that we were probably nowhere near the Galloping Dominos when the bombing took place, a good guess on her part.

After telling Cassandra what had gone down and letting her get an idea of what was publishable and what was not from the Fitch and Rice shooting, it was time to call Chicago.

"Dawn and Muriel are at Jacky's office," Cassandra said. "This can be one big conference call."

"We should bet before we call," Jimmy said. "How many times will Jacky call someone an asshole?"

We would have all lost our bets. Jacky was calm.

Muriel and Dawn not so calm.

Jacky kept saying "Jesus" a lot.

"Jesus, the equipment was stolen from there?"

Disappearing Act

And "Jesus, it does all of that?"

And "Jesus, I thought we were just running a popular magic show?"

Muriel kept interrupting with her favorite expletive. "Dumb sons of bitches, that's all those Feldsteins are, dumb sons of bitches. They tried to run the liquor business into the ground in Chicago. That's almost impossible to do, but they damn near did it. Dumb sons of bitches. I told Jacky they were dumb sons of bitches. Now, what do we have? We're out two million, and our magician is on the run from some goofy Korean son of a bitch and his *shvartzer* girlfriend. And that Braxton guy, another dumb son of a bitch. It's no wonder these people end up dead. I'm amazed they've lived so long."

My loving wife was economical.

"What kind of shit is this shit?"

And "Those two shits Jerry and Neal got into shit and brought shit to Art and left us with all this shit."

And "This golem shit maybe isn't shit we should take lightly."

"Jesus, another dimension," Jacky said.

"Jesus, Roswell."

"Jesus, atomic bomb testing."

"Government sons of bitches," Muriel said. "Lying sons of bitches."

"Ezekiel and golems," Dawn said. "This is heavy Jewish shit."

We finally got to practicalities.

"You and Jimmy keep nosing around," Jacky said. "Use your best judgment as to taking actions. I got Danny Flood looking at the agreements I signed at the Dominos. There's some sort of key man policies we hold on Art and Jerry Feldstein. I think we end up with a large chunk of dough on their passing. Muriel urged me to make sure we were covered. If Danny has to fly in, I'll let you know."

Lawyer Flood would be coming from LA. He had taken over some of the legal duties once handled by Jimmy, following Jimmy's "retirement."

"I'll be happy to guide him around," Jimmy said.

"Yeah, I don't know how familiar he is with Vegas," Jacky said. "And Cassandra, we need to put that Magic Carpet thing in your safe. We're going to hang onto it while we see what to do with it."

Dawn had something to add.

"You know the golems this guy Zeke keeps referring to?"

"Yeah, what about it?" Jacky asked.

"There's a famous golem story from Prague in the fifteen-hundreds," Dawn said. "The rabbi built a golem to defend the Prague ghetto from the emperor. The rabbi made it out of clay and brought it to life through incantations. The golem could make itself invisible and summon spirits from the dead. They decided that the golem shouldn't be active on the Sabbath. The rabbi would deactivate the golem on Friday evenings. One Friday evening, he forgot, and the golem went on a murderous rampage. The rabbi finally managed to immobilize it in front of the synagogue. They hid the golem's body in an attic of the synagogue where it could be restored to life when needed. They say that an SS storm trooper went into the attic during World War II and tried to destroy the golem, but he fell dead as he made the first swing with a hammer."

"How much of that is true?" Jimmy asked.

"It's a legend," Dawn said. "But it's a warning like the Frankenstein story or the Terminator story. We invent something to defend ourselves, and it ends up destroying us."

"We should all be cautious," Jacky said. "The old Jews and the old Italians weren't just pissing red wine."

Several minutes later, the conference call broke up. Jimmy and Cassandra headed for her office. I waited a couple of minutes and called Dawn's cell phone.

"I'm so glad you weren't hurt," she said. "This Vegas thing keeps getting crazier. We're all worried about you. Molly wants to know when Daddy's coming home. She wants to take you to the aquarium to see the fishes. Her pre-school went there today. She's next door visiting her friend Sarah at the Goldberg's house while I'm down at Jacky's."

"I miss you, too," I said. "It's the damnedest thing, I've been here a few days, and six people involved in this Charlemagne stuff are dead, and I've never had to pull my gun once. It's almost like what you described. The golem can become invisible and destroy at will."

We spoke for another ten minutes about Molly and what Dawn was doing for the museums she worked with. Antiquities were big. Everyone wanted a piece of the past. I wondered if it was due to the future being so frightening for some.

"Yes, Nick," she said. "I worry about the nightmare we're leaving our daughter."

I found Jimmy in Cassandra's office. He sat silent while Cassandra spoke on the phone.

"So, they ran them through all the databases and came up with nothing?" she asked. "It's like these birds never existed? The fingerprints don't match up with anyone's?"

She paused to listen.

"So, whoever Fitch and Rice were, all we know about their identity is that they're dead? No identity? Dead. Thanks, Roland. I'll get back at you."

She turned to where Jimmy and I sat.

"You heard it. For all we know, Fitch and Rice might as well have been golems."

"What about this Colonel Kim guy and his girlfriend?" I asked. "What's his story?"

Cassandra smiled.

"Big playboy type. Plenty of money. He thinks he can turn Pipes into a star. That'll be a good trick. She can croak out a song or two before the room clears out, but she must have other talents that keep the Colonel happy. She's beautiful, but not the sharpest knife in the drawer."

"She playing anywhere?" Jimmy asked. "We ever go see her? I don't remember her act if we did."

"I think that was the time you fell asleep," Cassandra said. "I'll try to get some info on where she's singing."

We decided to swing by Galloping Dominos to see what we could find in the aftermath of the bombing. We'd meet Cassandra later at Rusty's after she got done at the website.

Jimmy was happy to be on the road again, driving the big Caddy. He was another guy who sometimes thought better while behind the wheel.

"So, here's what I'm thinking," he said. "You don't go bombing Art and Jerry unless you have to get them out of the way. Now, why would you want them out of the way? If you're the rednecks, maybe it's because you're too stupid to figure anything out other than killing everyone until you find Zeke. This Colonel Kim guy, he's going to bomb them because, what, they fell asleep when Pipes was singing? This shit doesn't make sense."

We drove a few minutes in silence. Gears were turning in each of our heads.

"Moe, Curly, and Larry?" I asked. "What's their last name?"

"Sammy's guys?" Jimmy pulled the Caddy into a parking lot for a 7-11.

"Yeah," I said. "Is it Cavaretta?"

"Ralphie, Pete and Vito Cavaretta," Jimmy said. "One of them did time. I forget which one. Something about bombing some soul music hangout on Chicago's Southside."

The trunk of the Caddy had what we were looking for. The laptop from Fitch and Rice's suite at the Excalibur was wrapped in the old newspaper I took from Neal Braxton's closet.

CHAPTER TWENTY

The Galloping Dominos parking lot where the Feldsteins had met the wonders of C4 plastique was taped off while investigators looked for evidence and pieces of Jerry and Art. Security guards directed traffic to the South parking lot, or if you chose to have your classic ride destroyed by a hopped-up loser on speed, the valet parking line. Being careful consumers, we chose the parking lot.

We found Sammy Di Carlo sitting behind the desk once occupied by the late, great Neal Braxton. It was pretty much the way I had left it a day before. The smattering of Vegas brochures and flyers was more than enough literature to challenge the intellect of Sammy.

"Hah, what can I do for youse two guys?" He asked. "I can't rent youse a room. We don't cater to fairies. Hah."

"We're here to pay our respects to the widow Marcy," I said.

"She ain't here," Sammy said. "They're still picking up the pieces of Art and Jerry. I guess, as soon as they find enough pieces, they'll toss them into a casket and get them into the ground before sunset. That's the Jew way, ain't it?"

"Depends on how orthodox you want to be," I said. "Some sit shiva for a week, others not so much."

"Jesus, a week," Sammy said. "That's way too much Chivas for me. I'm more of a martini guy. You know, shaken not stirred. Me and James Bond. I heard there was a shooting at Dominic's right after we left. You guys piss in your pants?"

"Must have been right around the time Jerry and Art got killed." Jimmy said. "That gives you a pretty good alibi."

Sammy leaned his 300 pounds back in Braxton's designer swivel chair.

"Could've been anyone. Those things hook up to the ignition. Hell, could've been one of those valet jockeys. Besides, I liked Art. Jerry was okay, I guess. Not much in the cojones department, but he's gone now. So, what difference does it make?"

"So what?" I asked. "You got yourself a part-time job playing the part of Neal Braxton?"

He leaned forward and reached for a cigarette on the desk.

"I'm covering for my daughter. With those two gone, this whole joint falls to her. She inherits the whole thing."

"That's good to know," I said. "Now we know where to get the money that Jacky's been looking for. Jerry and lover boy Neal collected the two million from the magician's agent. They were working for the Dominos at the time. Guess who's going to make good on it?"

Sammy got red in the face.

"That's bullshit. How do you know they got it? That fag magician took it, and you can't find him, so you're lookin' for some fall guy."

"I'm looking at one right now. You thought it would be easy to stroll into Vegas and pop Braxton as he ran for his house. You heard there was a problem with Jacky getting paid, but you knew that Braxton and Jerry were holding back the dough. Marcy tipped you off that they had the dough hidden away. She was trying to find it before Jerry and Neal ran off together. So, one of the Cavaretta brothers, I'm saying it was Vito, plugged Braxton. I like him for it because he's been busted a couple of times for carrying without a license and threatening with a deadly weapon."

"Yeah, that's all bullshit." He leaned back and puffed on his cigarette.

"I also like Vito because he's never heard of a silencer," I said. "He put three slugs into Braxton and woke the whole neighborhood. That meant you boys couldn't go into the house and search it."

"More bullshit." He looked around the office as if checking for something.

"I figure Ralphie Cavaretta for the tricking out of Art's Mercedes," I said. "He goes back to that dispute you had with some of the Chicago brothers at the Black Cat Soul Station. I think he served five years for demolition without a contract on that one."

"Six years," Jimmy said. "They added one when they figured Ralphie couldn't count."

"Talkin' shit," Sammy said. "That's all you guys are good for, talkin' shit."

"Things got a little more complicated for you when you heard that some people were looking for the equipment the magician used in his show," I said. "Word got around once the magician split that Jerry and Neal had the equipment, too. Neal was dumb enough to go around showing off the coins that he thought was part of what the magician used in the show. That drew in a way bigger cast than you thought you'd be dealing with. Fitch and Rice were digging for the equipment, a couple of Russians were too, and so was the Confederate Front, headed by a guy named Ashley Beauregard. Remember him?"

"No, who's that?"

"He's only some yokel that had a hit record on your Country Cussin' label under the name Beau Ashley. It was called 'Blue-Eyed Confederate Lady.' You touched bases with him several times. At first, you told him you wanted him to get back to singing, but later, you told him you were on his side in bringing back the Confederacy."

"Yeah? Where's the proof of that?"

"You should be careful of where you're standing when someone from the newspaper takes a photo at the Confederate Front meeting in Boulder City. You should also be careful about what goes up on the Black Like Me Records website. You're pushing a singer named Pipes. There are photos of you with her and her main man Colonel Kim and a couple torpedoes that could match up well with the two hitters that took out Fitch and Rice."

"Fitch and Rice are dead?"

"You know damn well they are," I said. "You asked if we pissed in our pants at the Dominic's shooting, but you never asked about who got hit. Reason being that you had it set up. You knew."

"Why would I do that?"

"Because Fitch and Rice were in the way. They kept looking for the equipment where you didn't want them looking. You heard they had some of it, but not enough to do the kind of damage Kim was looking for. You figured if you could get Fitch and Rice out of the way and get the Confederate Front tossed in the can, you could deal with Colonel Kim. He spends a lot of money with you pushing Pipe's career, and you'd have a chance to help him get the equipment. If it's in Jerry or Art's house, you've got a shot at it. Plus, there's two million hanging around somewhere. Did you promise Kim you'd try to get Pipes into the vacant theater? By getting the Feldsteins out of the way, you could control a casino. Not bad for a slimy pile of shit from Calumet City."

"Yeah? So what? Where's the proof? Nice story. You're like they say in Texas, all cattle and no hat."

He had it ass-backward, of course, but no one jumped in to correct him. It was reeling him in time.

"So, this act of yours was so shaky that Jimmy and I figured it out in the car on the way here. Of course, being good citizens, we decided to alert the authorities about the tawdry nature of you and your three employees, the brothers Cavaretta."

"Bullshit." Sammy slumped in his chair.

"Detective Jake Glover and several of his officers have been talking with the Cavarettas. It turns out that Vito's gun could be a match up for the weapon that killed the guy whose chair you're sitting in. I guess being frugal on Vito's part means never having to say goodbye and tossing a gun into a dumpster. I suspect that Vito isn't the type to wash his hands after killing someone or taking a leak, for that matter, so there's probably gunshot residue there."

Sammy leaned forward in his chair.

"Here's how I see it. I don't keep the Cavarettas on my payroll. What they do is on their own. I know them, but I don't control them. You think you got it up on me? Like you're somehow better than me? Here's what I know, and I'll tell it to the cops. This disbarred lawyer and some punk out of Chicago came into my office and threatened to kill me if I didn't hand over two million bucks. They said they were the ones that killed the Feldsteins. I don't take any shit from punks."

His hand was quick as it came up from under the desk with the revolver. Jimmy ducked left. I dove right. A shot rang out. Then another came from behind us. I looked up. Sammy had blood all over his shirt. Another shot rang out from behind us. This one hit Sammy in the forehead as he went down.

"Piece of shit," someone said from behind us.

It was Detective Jake Glover.

"I believe you boys might be owing me a drink or two." He holstered his weapon.

CHAPTER TWENTYONE

Justice was quick, if somewhat imperfect. Sammy Di Carlo's body was still warm when Detective Duffy brought the handcuffed Cavaretta brothers into the office of the late Neal Braxton.

Detective Glover looked at Vito Cavaretta, then pointed down at the remains of Sammy.

"This is justice," Glover said. "It takes a shape of its own. Sometimes it's quick and satisfying. Sometimes it takes years and a lot of money to arrive at an outcome and everyone walks away pissed. We don't want that, do we?"

The Cavarettas looked at each other and shook their heads.

"Good," Glover said. "Di Carlo here copped to killing Braxton and planting the bomb in Feldstein's car. He then tried to kill these two gentlemen who were making inquiries about a past due bill the casino owes. Just as Di Carlo drew his revolver to fire, Detective Duffy and myself entered the room and managed to draw our weapons in time to stop Di Carlo from killing any further. You guys like that version so far?"

The Cavarettas nodded in unison.

"Good. It comes at a price."

"We talkin' just walk away, Jose?" Vito asked. He looked at his brothers, then at Glover.

"We could be."

Glover turned to Duffy.

"Bring what we took off these birds when we searched them."

Duffy came back with three plastic bags containing wallets, keys, rolls of cash and other personal items.

Disappearing Act

Glover reached into each bag and took out keys and a wallet. He grabbed all the cash out of the wallets and counted out a thousand dollars for each man and shoved the wallet, keys and thousand dollars into the shirt pocket of each. He took the gun from Vito's bag and wiped it clean then shoved it into Sammy's dead hand.

"Jesus," Vito said. "I had over twelve grand."

"Yeah, me too," Ralphie said.

Pete nodded agreement.

"Maybe you'd rather hire some shit lawyer and spend ten to life upstate with OJ's crew?" Glover said.

The three shook their heads.

"You boys know where the airport is," Glover said. "Drive there direct and get the first flight out. If you come back, I'll kill you."

Duffy took the cuffs off the Cavarettas and hustled them out toward their rental car.

Glover turned to Jimmy and me.

"Duffy has a couple affidavits for you two to sign, basically saying what I just said about Di Carlo fessing up and trying to kill you. We left out the part about how you entered Braxton's house unauthorized two times and left with whatever it was you took. I knew you'd be coming back when I saw you unlatch the door in the upstairs bedroom. By the way, you dropped an envelope marked 'Gibson Les Paul Guitar.' I kept it for sentimental reasons. I haven't wiped the prints off of it, yet."

I looked at Jimmy.

"Sounds good." Jimmy winked at me.

I remembered we wore the plastic gloves from Gus's Ribs while we poked around Braxton's.

"I'm okay, too." I said.

"I got to go now and give an exclusive to Cassandra's reporter out front," Glover said. "Duffy will give a handout to the rest of the media which they'll no doubt fuck up."

Jimmy and I walked down the hall to Marcy's office. It was dark and empty. I sat down at her desk and hit the space bar on her computer. An airline itinerary popped into view.

Disappearing Act

Her flight had left that morning at nine for Miami. I looked at my watch. According to her itinerary, she was already on her plane to Caracas.

I looked at her email. One was addressed to Jerry:

"I've had it with you and Art and this whole goddamn place. I found the money you held out from Jacky in your goddamn golf bag. I'm taking it and taking off. I'm tired of my sleaze ball uncle hanging around, too. He wanted me to put some phony producer named Kim in touch with Ted Evans, Charlemagne's manager. Like I should know where he's gone when no one else knows where he is. Jesus though, walking in on you and Neal Braxton was the worst. I don't ever want to see any of you again. Marcy."

Another was addressed to Colonel Kim;

"The only address we have for Ted Evans is Route Seven, Box 102 Clark County, NV."

Both emails went out at seven that morning.

I printed both emails and called Karen on her cell phone.

"Nick," she answered. "We're at the ballpark again, Can you guys make it? The game starts in an hour."

"By any chance is Tim umpiring?" I asked.

"He is and guess what? One of God's Witnesses came by Feel Da Dreams today and apologized. She said she was fed up with their shit. Her name's Carole and she's going to fill in tonight for Dani our shortstop. Dani has to work an extra shift at the theater."

I told her we were on the way.

This time we pulled up to the Dykes bench with four pizzas and four cases of beer in four cheap plastic coolers. We felt generous. We had already pissed away the proceeds of a Gibson Les Paul guitar by dropping an envelope while fleeing Neal Braxton's house. It was a nice tip for Detective Glover. It would help fund his research into Las Vegas happy hours.

We arrived between games. The Smoke Eaters had just played a team from Sunrise Medical Center, the X-rays. The Dykes were slated to play a team from Sonny's Go For Broke Lounge, the Dealers.

I saw Tim standing off to the side, taking a break between games. I brought him a cold one.

Disappearing Act

"Thanks, Nick," he said. "You're better than one of those Saint Bernards that find people frozen on the mountains."

"I may need your help with something," I said. "If I give you an address on the FedEx route, can you tell me where it might be and if there's any kind of a delivery going there either today or sometime this week?"

I showed him the last message from Marcy.

"Let me make a call, Nick."

He stepped away.

Karen strolled over to me and took a shirt out of a plastic bag.

"I hope I got your size right," she said.

The front had the Vegas Dykes logo and on the back was printed "Nick."

I looked over to the bench where a group of Dykes stood eating pizza. The one with "Jimmy" on the back was eating a slice and talklng law with Marlene.

Tim came back from his call and handed me the paper with Marcy's message on it.

"Nothing going out there today or tomorrow, unless it's one of those same day deliveries," he said. "I can monitor that address for you and let you know, if you want."

"That would be great," I said. "It's real important. You ever been out that way on a delivery?"

"Couple times with a driver that knew the territory, but I could probably find it on my own. That's all desert out there and some of the roads wash out in a heavy rain, so what looks like it did last week could be a lot different if you went out there today."

The Dealers were not like the Witnesses. They were into having a good time, win or lose. They joked with each other when someone would strike out on their team and they were quick to compliment a nice catch by the Dykes.

In the fourth inning, I walked. The Dealers first baseman came over and stood near the bag.

"I really don't know how to ask this, so I guess I'll just stumble in," he said. "I know you're not a dyke, but you're a Dyke. How'd you get to be a Dyke?"

"I've been asking myself that," I said. "It had nothing to do with clean living."

Disappearing Act

We laughed. He slapped me on the back and said, "Hey, I stole one of your beers before the game. Stop into Sonny's sometime and it's all on me."

The game went into the seventh inning, tied at five. Jimmy got to second base, the result of two errors. Marlene came up to bat with two outs. She whacked the first pitch deep down the left field line, foul. The left fielder tossed the ball back to the pitcher. I felt a large raindrop in my arm, then another. I looked toward the outfield fence and could barely see it. A downpour was rushing in.

"Time," Tim yelled. "Rain delay. Get to shelter."

Water flooded the field. Players took refuge where they could.

We stood under the tin roofed dugout drinking beers and eating rain-drenched pizza for an hour. Finally, Tim told us it was all over.

"We'll just make this one a tie in the books," he said.

We said our goodbyes and headed toward Rusty's to meet Cassandra.

We had answers to some of our questions and at least one of them wasn't going to make Jacky happy. The two million bucks were landing in Caracas with Marcy Feldstein. From what Jimmy and I could put together, it seemed that there also might be a problem using the theater at Galloping Dominos for anything.

"Christ, the owners are dead, and the heiress has fled the country with someone else's money," Jimmy said. "The emails and the reservations on the Internet are confessions of guilt. No owners, no heiress, the joint could go into receivership. If you think Jacky pisses and moans over the way Muriel spends money, wait till you hear him react to this one. The only thing that will brighten his day is that Sammy Di Carlo is dead. Pain in the ass that one was."

The wipers on the Caddy did their best getting us through the rain. A convertible ahead of us, had four soaked tourists trying to figure out how the top worked.

"Hey, it's a rental," I yelled as we passed by.

"Everyone's got troubles," Jimmy said. "You think those Confederate Front assholes are dumb enough to take the fall for killing Fitch and Rice?"

"I might be able to find out," I said.

Disappearing Act

I phoned Roland Rivers.

"Jesus, Nick," he answered. "You okay? I heard from Cassandra that you and Jimmy Cox were at Dominic's when the shooting went down. You guys like living dangerously?"

I looked at the two of us in the front seat of the Caddy. We were soaked to the skin, wearing Vegas Dykes shirts with beer and pizza spots on the front.

"We're just two debonair gents enjoying the cultural opportunities in Vegas," I said. "We were also front row center when Sammy Di Carlo bought it at Galloping Dominos."

"Jesus. Is there someplace you guys go to order tickets for these things? You guys okay?"

"Yeah, we're wondering about the three guys they picked up in the Dominic's shooting. What's going on there?"

"Someone gave an anonymous tip that the two victims at Dominic's had a suite at the Excalibur. The cops went over there and found fingerprints on the door that matched Ashley Beauregard's. That shook up the Confederates a bit, but the guns they retrieved from the three at the lounge downstairs didn't match up with the vics at Dominic's. The cops leaned on the three of them pretty hard. Where were the guns they used? They'd all go down together, unless someone came forward with information that would put the case solved."

"The old let's make a deal and one of you will walk as a material witness game," Jimmy said.

"That you Jimmy?" Roland asked.

"Yeah, we're on speaker. We're coming back from the ballpark."

"Is it true you guys are playing for a lesbian softball team?"

"Playing and winning, although tonight was a tie due to the rain."

"You can't win them all. Anyway, one of the Confederates rolled on the other two. Ashley Beauregard copped to an illegal weapons charge. He'll serve a year in a minimum facility in exchange for giving up his two amigos. He told the cops where they held a cache of weapons in Boulder City. Among the goodies were surface to air hand-held missiles and automatic weapons on the forbidden list. Apparently, Beauregard is willing to state that Junior and Clem were somewhere out of his sight when the shooting went down at Dominic's and they talked a lot of shit about Fitch and Rice before the shooting."

"What's your take on it?" I asked.

"Hey Nick, I'm not qualified to make a judgment. I barely know how to make an anonymous tip, but if those day-glow Aloha shirts they had on when they were busted is any indicator, I'd say they're cooked. I go for the Tommy Bahama brand myself."

"Good man," Jimmy said.

"I'm gonna have to ring off soon," Roland said. "I'm at a strategy meeting pushing the new sewer bonds and street lighting tax. A couple of my construction people are looking for contracts. Lots of jobs there, lots of votes."

We let him go when he started describing the finer points of sales tax and debenture bonds. To me, it sounded like Jimmy's complicated bet on the Blackhawks.

The jukebox at Rusty's was playing Sinatra again as we walked in. This time it was a fitting theme for Marcy Feldstein, "Come Fly with Me." We headed for the booth where Cassandra sat.

We filled her in on our version of the events of the day, featuring the shootings of Fitch and Rice and Sammy Di Carlo and the bomb crater under what had been Art Feldstein, his son Jerry and a year-old Mercedes.

Cassandra licked some salt from the margarita she was drinking.

"One of these days you two are going to shock the Hell out of me by just hanging out at the pool working on your tans or going to the movies. What's the body count today? Five? And you know what gets me is that neither one of you fired a shot."

Jimmy and I sipped our beers and smiled at her.

"Go ahead charm your way into my heart," she said.

"Aw, Cassie," Jimmy said. He hugged her.

"Jimmy, not 'Cassie', that's only for our special times," she said.

"I didn't hear a thing," I said. "I turned off my hearing when Roland started describing sewer contracts to us."

We laughed.

"It was a good day for the website," she said. "We have the Fitch and Rice shootings on the front page next to the bombing at

Disappearing Act

Dominos and the wonderful heroism of Detective Glover resulting in the death of dear old Sammy. We even dug up some of his old singers who were more than happy to toss dirt on his grave. I think he managed to cheat everyone he signed to one of his labels."

"And the fact that one of his old singers took a minor part of the rap for Fitch and Rice makes dear old Sammy seem like a one-man crime wave," Jimmy said.

"There are a few complications, however," Cassandra said. "I've talked with Jacky since our conference call and after you called from Dominos to let me know that Marcy had run with the two mil."

"I bet he was ready to chew the carpet," I said.

"No, he was pretty okay with it. In fact, he was happy."

"What? Happy that Sammy bought it?"

"No, Jacky is the new owner of the Galloping Dominos. Art had everything going to Jerry when he died. Jerry had no will, but he did have a pre-nup with Marcy saying she got his life insurance, but nothing else. So, it all went to Harry, Art's brother in Miami, but when the papers were signed buying the liquor company in Chicago, Harry and Jacky made a separate agreement. Harry got the two-bedroom condo on Collins Avenue in exchange for transferring any and all claims on the Dominos to Muriel and Jacky. Danny Flood says it's a lock."

"If Danny says it, I believe it," Jimmy said. "Any other complications?"

"Hooker Doris is upset about something. She wants to meet with both of you at the breakfast bar in the morning at nine. Something happened to her as a result of her encounter with Fitch and Rice. She'll explain it."

"Jesus, if it's a lawsuit, how do you sue two dead spooks," Jimmy said. "Nobody even knows their real names."

"One other thing," Cassandra said. "I found out where Pipes is playing. If you boys want to do a quick change of clothes, we can catch her show. It's out at the Short Cut Back Beat Lounge."

"Is Colonel Kim going to be there?" I asked.

"And probably his two torpedoes, too," she said.

"Jesus, that joint's a real dump," Jimmy said.

"Well, then you boys will feel right at home," Cassandra said.

The Short Cut Back Beat Lounge was a biker bar that had gone downhill. If I had to guess, I would have pegged it as a scuzz bar aspiring for flophouse status. We sat on stools at the bar. The showroom held about thirty small tables that would hold four drinks and nothing more, or the nodded-out head of someone who had way too much. Four of the tables were so occupied with sleepers. The bar had a patina of stickiness that made you want to order three beers, no glasses.

Colonel Kim sat off to one side of the small stage. He wore what looked like an old school blazer with an ascot and a silk shirt. Reflective aviator sunglasses and a cigarette holder with a small black cigar stuck in it completed the portrait of a tin horn dictator who had somehow fallen off the screen at a Jackie Chan movie.

We arrived just as Pipes was about to begin her first song. A tired piano player spoke into the microphone full of feedback and announced that, "Direct from an exciting West Coast engagement, please welcome the one and only Pipes."

About fifteen people in the room were sober enough to clap as Pipes stepped up to the microphone. She was a beautiful woman with a fine figure and a pleasant face that beamed warmth, but unfortunately, no voice.

First, she destroyed the Stones' "You Can't Always Get What You Want," then Bob Seger's "Night Moves." She was about to start another song when one of the head-down-on-the-table drunks leaned back and shouted, "Shit, you sure can't get what you want around here. How much you charge for a few night moves in the backroom, Soul Bunny?"

It wasn't instant, but it was thorough. The Colonel's two torpedoes approached from each side of the drunk. They weren't wearing their day-glow Aloha shirts or their cowboy hats now, but they fit the part for the shooting at Dominic's. They each took an arm of the drunk and dragged him backwards toward the door. One gut punch and one to the chin sailed the drunk out the swinging doors where he fell into a parking lot puddle.

Colonel Kim stood up from his nearby table and grabbed Pipes.

"We leaving this shit house right now," he said. "These people don't know good music when they see it. This whole Vegas place full of shit. Should burn to ground, one day soon. No more."

They were gone, leaving the piano player alone who promptly played a medley of Gershwin tunes. It wasn't much to look at, but it sounded good.

We drank up and decided to call it a night.

"I believe you boys might be losing your mojo," Cassandra said as we walked to the car. "That's two bars we've been in tonight and no one's gotten shot."

I got back to my room at the Bellagio just after midnight. Two messages were on the room phone. Both Dawn and Jacky wanted to talk "any time of the night."

Jacky answered on the first ring.

"Hell of a day, Nick. You know that the Galloping Dominos is ours? You talked with Cassandra about what Danny Flood had set up on the liquor deal? You know that Harry Feldstein is out, and we're in?"

I pictured Jacky picturing me nodding as he asked all the questions and not giving me pause to answer.

"Good," he said in response to my non-response. "I want you to know that I have every confidence in you and Jimmy and Cassandra to get things under control on your end of the project. I'm sending Cohen and Collins tomorrow to take over the books at the Dominos. The joint was just making it under Art and Jerry. As far as that piece of shit Marcy goes, we won't worry. Danny says we can try putting a lien on her insurance policy she has coming from Jerry."

"Sounds good," I finally got a word in.

"This thing with this guy Old Zeke, or whatever he calls himself? He used this special equipment to produce the show, right? He's still got what he used, right? Well, I think we had something there, you know? A money-maker? Right?"

I was getting tired of nodding my head, but Jacky was excited, and when he got excited, you had to listen.

"So, you know Gene Cornell, and how he always wanted us to get involved in producing big rock shows, horse shows, dog shows, and God, I don't know what the Hell? The man's a dynamo."

I thought about what he was saying as he sped forward in his excited rap. I was now playing a guessing game with him to see if I knew where this was going. Gene Cornell was a promoter, born Yevgeny Kornakova. He had long ago hot-footed it out of Mother Russia and started hustling the minute he hit the great USA. He began with small bands, some folk acts, and some small festivals he created. Lately, he was riding high with his discovery Bobbi Jo Wallis, who had won the top prize on North America Makes Music.

Cohen and Collins were two other characters of note. They were roommates at Notre Dame who had formed an accounting firm upon graduating. Then they executed a maneuver designed to keep wealth in their families. They married each other's sisters, and each had half a dozen kids. I could never get it straight who had converted to which religion. They were both capable of doing the Woody Allen misunderstood shmuck act as well as making pilgrimages to Notre Dame to see the Fighting Irish play football. It was further confusing because one of their kids was always getting bar mitzvah-ed or making their first holy communion, which meant Nick and Dawn dressing up and dropping a c-note on the little devil. I always suspected that some of the kids were doing both ceremonies.

I tuned back into what Jacky was saying.

"So, Gene goes way back to these two guys that used to run the Moscow Circus..."

"You don't mean Boris and Alexi, do you?" I cut in.

"Uh, yeah. I uh..."

"We had drinks together a couple days ago," I said. "Right here at the Bellagio. They drive around here in a Mustang convertible."

"Jesus, Nick. You're amazing. Do you think they might be interested in doing something with us? We need to get that theater back in business. Cash flow. Cohen and Collins. That's what they always say."

"Alexi and Boris are staying at a private club out in the desert," I said, preferring not to name the whorehouse on the card they gave me.

"You and Jimmy should meet with them and maybe get in touch with that Old Zeke guy. Let's see if we can put something together. I'll tell Gene to hold off for now. We'll bring him in later, maybe."

Disappearing Act

In the background, I could hear Muriel's voice.

"Jesus, Jacky. Come to bed already. Nick needs some sleep, too."

"Did you hear my boss in the background?" Jacky said. "I guess we'll call it a night. Stay in touch. Do what you have to, Nick."

He was gone.

I did a quick check of my blood pressure, popped a Norvasc, and called Dawn.

"Nick, are you checking your blood pressure?" she asked. "You're doing a lot of running around with Jimmy. You must be tired. I wish you were at home. Hell, I wish I was there. I'd love to see Celine and Cher. Maybe I could come out?"

I told her about my blood pressure and said I missed her and Molly. She laughed when I told her about the Pipes concert, not exactly Celine or Cher. Jimmy and I playing for the Dykes brought more smiles –yes, I can tell when my wife is smiling over the phone – she purrs, and only I can hear her.

"You're finding real people out there, Nick. Everyone always thinks that Vegas is full of phonies and bull shitters. Maybe it's just you, Nick. You bring out the best in people. You bring out the best in me."

They were kind words to sleep on. We said good night. I had the desk send a wake-up at seven, and I went to sleep.

I was up at 6:30 and in the shower. Something was telling me that this was a busy day about to happen. The only thing on the schedule was breakfast with Hooker Doris at nine. Jimmy and I would handle that, whatever it was that was bothering her. Later, I'd get hold of Boris and Alexi. Jimmy would get a kick out of meeting them.

But still, I felt uneasy. Something was looming, like a thunderstorm just over the horizon. It was a feeling that wouldn't go away. I checked the Glock. The magazine was full. I had another full one in my pocket.

I poured some room service coffee and watched the early news—the shooting at Dominic's led. Mug shots of Ashley, Clem, and Junior were featured. Then came the photo of Sammy and the story from Dominos with shots of what was left of Art's Mercedes. Video from some of the acts that Sammy had under contract followed. Next was an interview with one of his R&B singers, Satchel Marvin.

Satchel said, "I always knew that Sammy Di Carlo was a mother bleep and a real piece of bleep, but him bombing those poor mother bleep and tryin' to shoot those fellas and gettin' involved with those redneck bleepholes. Man, he ain't nothin' but bleep."

Detective Glover gave a short statement that justice had been done, and the news moved on to a series of convenience store robberies that had happened overnight. The perps wore Halloween masks. Security cam video from outside one of the stores showed the geniuses staring right at the lens before putting their masks on and entering the store.

The weather was next. A guy who could have been a used car salesman on speed did a three-minute report in about thirty seconds—low pressure forming over mountains, a chance of rain later, maybe an inch, maybe nothing. Radar swept along, looking at cloud cover. Or was it false echoes? Or possibly incoming missiles? Whatever it was, it was worth a commercial for air conditioning your home and solar heating your pool.

I had done my hand laundry routine before retiring, and now I was faced with which fashion choice to make. Should I go all kinky and wear my Vegas Dykes shirt, or should I announce my belief in lost causes by wearing my Cubs shirt? As I was about to grab for one, my cell phone rang.

"Nick, I hope I didn't wake you up. It's Tim, your friendly umpire FedEx guy."

"Not to worry," I said. "The forces of justice never sleep, so I have to stay one step ahead of them."

We laughed.

"That address from last night. My friend Paul called to tell me there's a late afternoon delivery going out there. A package addressed to Ted Evans from a Colonel Jae Joo Kim."

"That was quick," I said. "Think last night's downpour changed the roads out there?"

"Hard to say, but I hear there's another bit of rain on the way."

"I need to get out there later today. If I rent a four-wheel-drive vehicle, could you do the driving? I'd be willing to pay a couple hundred bucks if you're free to do it?"

"Yeah, I'm up for it."

I told him I'd get back to him with the rental info and where to meet.

Minutes later, I had a tan SUV lined up for noon pick up. We'd be making our trip to the desert looking like the Feds. Of course, I'd be wearing my Cubs shirt.

It was still early for breakfast with Jimmy and Hooker Doris. I was about to take in another helping of Vegas violence on the Channel 20 news when my room phone rang.

"Mister Nick. Alexi from Moscow Circus. I am hoping not I wake you up?"

"No, it's okay, Alexi," I said. "What can I do for you?"

"We hear all about Galloping Dominos and Art and Jerry, yeah. Too bad, no?"

"Yeah, too bad."

"But good news Mister Jacky the new owner, yes?"

"How did you hear about that, Alexi?"

"Gene Cornell talking with Mister Jacky in Chicago. He gives us your number."

"You're not talking about Yevgeny Kornakova, are you?"

"Used to be Yevgeny, but Putin pissed at him over not giving kickback on admissions to circus, so what do you know? Next thing he Gene Cornell in Chicago running talent agency."

"Yeah, I hear he has a star on North America Makes Music. Is he representing you boys, too?"

"Hard to describe relation. He marry to Boris daughter Anastasia. They have four kids, house in Evanston. We help when we can."

"I know what it's like," I said. "My wife and I have a two-year-old daughter."

We did the conversational back and forth, both of us slowly realizing that we had been given orders to put something together with Old Zeke. Would it be another Charlemagne? Or the Vegas version of the Moscow Circus? Maybe it would be a combination, but whatever it would be, it had better make money.

I put him on hold for a minute while I called Jacky to confirm.

"Nick. Glad you called. Has Alexi talked to you? Listen, we got to get that Zeke guy to do a show at the Dominos. He can do all the tech work. Gene and I can work out the financials here in Chicago. I don't know, maybe we'll come out, but you guys work together. Alexi and Boris used to run that Moscow Circus. Get together. Talk to the Old Zeke guy. We need a show that pulls money into the operation. Use whatever you can."

He finally shut up for a minute.

"Jimmy and I are going out there to see Zeke later this afternoon," I said. "There's some Korean hotshot arms dealer that's after Zeke for his toys. There are two components that, when put together, can make some kind of superweapon. This Colonel Kim guy needs to be excused from the party, or he'll ruin it for everyone."

"You do what you have to," Jacky said. "We're not trying to start a war. We just want a money-maker. Take the Russians with you. Gene tells me they're old friends with Zeke."

I told him we'd do our best and rung off.

Alexi liked the idea of renting an SUV and following us out to Zeke's. We'd meet at the rental place at noon.

A quick call caught Jimmy as he was kissing Cassandra goodbye. I explained our new marching orders and that I'd meet him at the Breakfast Bar.

"This is all a plot to drive me nuts," he said.

"Wait 'til you meet Hooker Doris," I said.

CHAPTER TWENTY-TWO

Hooker Doris sat at a table in the back of the Breakfast Bar. She smiled and waved at us as we entered. We sat down on each side of her. She was dressed in her Wendy's lookalike costume.

"I know Nick," she said to Jimmy. "You must be Cassandra's man. I'm Doris Day."

Jimmy looked at her as if she had just exploded out of a genie's magic lamp.

"Did you say that you're Doris Day?"

"Yes, it's on my driver's license and birth certificate. I'm not the one who did Pillow Talk. Her last name is really Kappelhoff. I do a different brand of pillow talk."

Jimmy smiled.

"I think you've charmed him into a trance," I said.

We laughed.

"Breakfast is on me," she announced. "I'm having the Long Shot Louie. It's a stack of waffles with Canadian bacon, blueberry ice cream with whipped cream, and a mimosa on the side."

The waitress came for our orders.

"I'm having what she's having," Jimmy said, "And he's having what I'm having because I'm not doing this without him."

"Yes, three Long Shot Louie's," Doris said, "And bring us all coffees."

A busboy arrived with coffee and water.

"I'm so glad you could come," Doris said. "I need someone who understands what that magic carpet ride of Fitch and Rice might have done to me. There's no getting hold of them now that they're dead. Cassandra tells me they were the ones shot at the betting parlor."

"Yeah, for sure," Jimmy said. "Nick and I were there when it went down. We hit the floor when those two guys walked in and started firing."

"Oh, my."

She looked around the room full of conventioneers and tourists. She looked back at me.

"Last time we talked I wasn't giving you the whole story about the magic carpet ride. Remember I said I saw another me on another magic carpet? We were both naked, and when I said something, she would try to say it too, but it came out garbled?"

I nodded.

"Well, it didn't just end there with me falling off the carpet and leaving with their toys. Fitch wanted to have sex with the other me. Rice wanted me. For a while, it was interesting watching Fitch do the other me doggie style while Rice tried his best Fido on me. I never get aroused on these dates, but I have a few standard lines that urge the customers on like, 'Oh, that's so nice,' and 'Such a big man, give me more.'"

Our orders arrived at that point. Doris ate some of her waffles and continued.

"As I was urging Rice on, my double across the room was mouthing the same lines I was using. Only they were coming out distorted, kind of like snarls and growls that kept getting louder, no matter how softly I was expressing myself. Rice finally finished with me, and I got dressed. That's when they started in that they weren't going to pay me because now they had a whore of their own just like me and they didn't need me. They had what they called a golem they had created using me as the model."

"What then?" Jimmy asked.

"They were really stoned on coke. They fell into a laughing fit. I grabbed their toys – the equipment they used for the magic carpet – and I grabbed their wallets. I left them with their new whore, the golem. Later we straightened out the money at the jail with Roland and Estelle. I never saw them after that."

There was more to come. I ate some of the waffles and Canadian bacon.

"I keep getting some sort of déjà vu from you," she said to Jimmy. "We've never…"

Disappearing Act

"No," Jimmy said. "I feel it, too. Maybe we're long-lost relatives."

She patted Jimmy on the hand and sipped some coffee.

"Yesterday afternoon, I had another date at New York, New York," she said. "A couple from Boston. They were easy to figure out. He'd leave the bedroom for a while. His wife and I would get it on together until we were both acting like we were desperate for a man with a stiff cock, then he'd come in and have his way with both of us. It's a simple scenario, almost boring, actually."

"Maybe you could give it a number," Jimmy said. "You know, the old 27b."

"Yes, but there was a bit of a snag in this 27b," Doris said. "To pull it off so that it can earn a major tip, my role is to be super-expressive. Like he's the best lover anyone has ever had. I told you I can blush on command, well I can fake a pretty good orgasm when I have to, with tears, drooling, loss of breath, you name it."

"I'll bet you can," I said.

"I really got going," Doris said. "That's when a naked intruder came rushing out of the bathroom, growling everything I was carefully expressing to lover man. The golem was back, and she scared Hell out of the three of us. The mood was lost. The guy thought he was being robbed. I tried to settle him down. 'No charge,' I said. 'Freebie. God, you made me come. She's my crazy sister.' I chased her into the bathroom with a golf club the guy had. I grabbed my clothes off the dresser. The wife had run screaming to the living room. The guy ran after her. I got dressed in the bathroom. The golem was gone. I grabbed my stuff and left."

"This never happened before?" Jimmy asked.

"No, but that was the first time I was back at New York, New York, since being there with Fitch and Rice. Did I activate the golem? Or is the golem running around the hotel creating sexual havoc?"

"You don't think it followed you out of there somehow?" I asked.

"I don't know. That's the real question. I told you, Nick. I'm ready to give up hooking. What happens if I find some guy I really want to be with? Is some monster going to come running out of the bathroom naked and growling?"

It was a question neither Jimmy nor I could answer, but we thought we knew someone who could. We'd finish breakfast and take Doris over to Cassandra's office, where we would have the conference room with the speakerphone.

Doris took a c note out of her purse and tossed it on the check as we stood. The waitress picked it up and said, "I'll get your change."

"It's all yours," Doris said. She pulled a black beret out of her purse and put it on her head. Jimmy stared at her as if he'd seen a ghost.

"Something wrong?" she asked.

"No, no." A smile came back to his face. "I was thinking about what you said about quitting what you're doing. I had to do that with lawyering not too long ago. So far, so good. Life is actually better. If I can help you, Cassandra, too, she'll help."

"She's a great role model," Doris said.

"We agree on most things," Jimmy said. "She thinks I'm crazy, and I know I am."

We laughed and headed for the Caddy.

Cassandra sat with us in the conference room at her office. Zeke was on the speakerphone. He had listened to Doris and said he might be able to do something.

"I don't have the toys that Fitch and Rice used," Zeke said. "But I think I could work around it. I had problems with golems with the equipment I have. Can you come out?"

"What are your roads like?" I asked. "Did the storm last night do any damage?"

"Yeah, a little. Do you have an SUV with all-wheel drive?"

"We do. We're picking it up at noon and heading out."

"Good, there's more rain due later today."

"You haven't had any trouble with intruders?"

"No, John's teaching me the finer points of shooting beer cans with an old Remington. We shot a couple rats, but none of the two-legged variety."

We rang off. Jimmy and I walked Cassandra to her office.

"We need the toys out of your safe," I said. "We want Zeke to look at all the equipment together and see if any kind of show can be put together for the Galloping Dominos. Our two Russian friends, Alexi and Boris, will be coming out with us, part of a deal

Jacky worked out with Gene Cornell. They were involved in the Moscow Circus."

"Things are moving fast," She said. "Sounds like Jacky's worried. Are Cohen and Collins coming out?"

"Tomorrow," Jimmy said.

"And Doris?" Cassandra asked.

"We're taking her out to see Zeke. It may be the only way to free her from her golem," I said. "Also, Colonel Kim and his torpedoes will be trailing a FedEx truck out there trying to find Zeke. We've got to get there before they do."

She shook her head and opened the safe.

"If you put these toys together with Zeke's, you get a superweapon. That's what Kim is after."

"Zeke's the only one who knows how to put the toys together," I said. "Fitch and Rice never understood what they had. As far as Kim goes, let's hope he's as good at stealing weapons as he is at picking singers."

She turned to face us. She was about to cry.

"Jimmy, make sure you take your golf bag," she said.

She handed me the "Welcome to Las Vegas" bag that held the Fitch and Rice toys. A tear made its way down her left cheek

Jimmy stepped forward and hugged her.

"Jay-jay, baby," she said. "Be careful, baby."

"Cassie. Cassie. Cassie."

"Jay-jay," Cassandra said. "Doris looks like your Rachel."

"I know. I know."

They held each other tight, rocking back and forth.

I walked toward the conference room, thinking about Dawn and Molly. Life was precious and fragile.

A fanatic offended by bare-headed women and laughter was somewhere out there planning his next massacre. He'd carry on his crusade by killing artists and wine drinkers. His weapons would come down a pipeline from creeps like Colonel Kim.

Some of his victims would be daughters named Rachel.

CHAPTER TWENTY-THREE

We drove toward the SUV rental place. Doris sat between Jimmy and me in the front seat of the Caddy. She had definite opinions about famous horses, particularly Derby winners, which got Jimmy interested. It gave me a chance to tune out what they were saying and tune in to my own thoughts.

I had been in Vegas for only a few days. Seven people who were involved in what I had come to investigate were dead. Three were in jail. A casino had changed hands, and a manager had run off to Caracas with two million bucks that didn't belong to her.

Was it me? Was I the catalyst that made this happen? Nick, the fifth horseman of the Apocalypse who accidentally brings mayhem to town in the form of a few questions and wisecracks?

My thoughts went like this:

My showing up at Braxton's office got Neal and Jerry to speed up their plans to take it on the lam. Marcy got wind of this and told her daddy. Sammy Di Carlo was already in the hunt for the magician and his goodies. Sammy planned to deliver the toys to the highest bidder, either the Confederate Front or Colonel Kim. Both knew Sammy through his record labels.

Sammy told both parties that Nick brought Chicago heat into the game. The Confederates put Jeff Davis on Nick's tail, and Davis ended up under the bus. Word got back to Neal and Jerry that Nick wasn't playing around. He was tossing people under tour coaches. That night Sammy and the Cavarettas took out Neal Braxton. Sammy also realized that Fitch and Rice were in the hunt. He got Colonel Kim to take out Fitch and Rice, but make it look like the Confederates did it. Sammy knew that Kim had way more money than the Confederates. He also knew it would be easy to take out Jerry and Art and have his daughter inherit the Galloping Dominos.

Suppose that Nick never showed his face in Vegas?

Do Neal and Jerry end up in Panama with Jacky's money, leaving Art and Marcy holding the bag? Would Jeff Davis still be alive?

I had to stop. I was starting to think like one of Jimmy's complicated bets. Whatever had happened as a result of my coming to Vegas, was in the past. There was no going back. It was like what Zeke was talking about at the Busted Flush. Maybe in an alternate reality, Neal and Jerry were in Panama with Jacky's money. Maybe I was home walking with Dawn and Molly along Lake Shore Drive.

What had happened got us to where we were now. Where we went from here was what I needed to concentrate on now. I was pissed at Jacky for expecting us to put everything back together. Like we were in some Agatha Christie mystery where the butler takes the rap, and everyone goes back to sipping sherry. I was betting that Alexi and Boris felt the same about Gene Cornell. It was easy to sit in the Pump Room at the Chicago Hotel and make deals.

Boris and Alexi were waiting at the rental place. They wore Khaki shorts and camo shirts. A Crocodile Dundee hat on each made it look like they were ready to shoot tigers, should there be any in the Great American Desert. Further reinforcing this notion was the AK-47 Boris carried.

"Is souvenir of Russia," Boris said. "Could be snakes in garden, no?"

"Piss on snake," Alexi said. "No need for gun. I strangle snake like Indiana Jones."

Tim pulled up to the rental place. After intros all around, Jimmy and Doris took him into the office to get him registered as one of the drivers.

I turned to my two Russian friends.

"Any ideas how we're going to pull this off?"

"Play by ear," Alexi said. "Maybe he throw us all out. Tell us all go to Hell."

"Nyet, nyet," Boris said. "Use charm. Tell him Nick dying of cancer and my grandkids going to live in orphanage because he won't do show at Dominos."

"I should tell you that there's a Colonel Kim and a couple of his boys that are coming out later to try to grab the equipment from Zeke. He thinks he can peddle the equipment to some terrorists or even North Korea or the Taliban."

"Oh, now you tell," Boris said. "This the same asshole with soul sister with lousy voice?"

"You know about him?"

"Hey, we hanging around here for maybe three weeks trying to get magician. We looking for other acts for Gene to save mortgage on house in Evanston. What you think? We born tomorrow?"

"Other day on strip, you say Immigration asking about Russians," Alexi said. "Night before we tell Kim that we help Pipes get visa. He tell us Pipes in country illegally from Congo. No sweat. Gene fix with Chicago congressman. Then we hear Pipes sing…"

"Da," Boris cut in. "Tell Nick how fast Mustang moves out of the parking lot. I thinking he drive us to Phoenix to get away from noise pollution."

The door to the rental office opened, and our trio stepped out. Doris was bubbling with laughter between Jimmy and Tim. She had a hand around each of their arms as she skipped along between them.

"Jimmy bringing daughter and boyfriend to see Zeke?" Alexi asked.

"Tim knows the roads out there where Zeke lives," I said. "There may be a few problems with washouts from the rain. There might be more rain on the way later today."

Jimmy walked up to where we stood talking.

"We're taking three vehicles as it turns out," he said. "This guy's got a used Hummer for rent. I always wanted to drive one. Nick and I will follow along. I'm going to toss my stuff into it. Tim knows the way, and Doris has a good map to help him."

"You have nice looking daughter," Alexi said.

"Uh, well, I uh guess I do," Jimmy stammered. "Nick, come give me a hand with my shit."

We walked over to the Caddy and opened the trunk.

"I want the golf bag," Jimmy said. "And I want the Butch Cassidy Realty signs."

Disappearing Act

I grabbed the golf bag.

"You want to come clean about the Hummer?" I asked. "Is this your Schwarzenegger coming out? Or are you losing yourself in a fantasy? You heard what Alexi said. You have a nice-looking daughter."

"And Tim better do right by her," Jimmy said. "Goddamn it, Nick, those two like each other. They don't need the two of us bothering them. Besides, what if Jacky calls us? I don't want to have to share any of his crap with them."

He was right. I shut up.

I had been with him in Chicago when the news came over the TV in the bar. A Parisian sidewalk restaurant had been attacked by terrorists. Jimmy's wife, Martha, and their daughter Rachel were on a cultural tour of France when they were killed.

Jimmy was a mess for weeks afterward. Jacky kept someone with him 24/7. I was single at the time, so I caught most of the duty. We drank too much and got into bar fights, taking out our anger on white-collar drunks who had their own rage issues.

Jacky finally got Jimmy into live-in counseling at a clinic outside Elkhorn, Wisconsin. I was excused from Jimmy watch and rewarded with a couple weeks chasing billfish in the Bahamas and the Florida Keys. I remembered his pain and how deeply it cut him. If he wanted to have Rachel back by being close to Doris, who was I to argue?

We were ready. Butch Cassidy Realty signs were on each side of the Hummer. Jimmy's Springfield rifle was out where we could grab it.

Tim pulled the lead vehicle out of the lot, followed by Alexi and Boris. We were the tail car.

We drove for half an hour and started to leave the metro area. My cell phone rang. It was from Tim. More accurately, it was Tim's phone with Doris talking.

"Tim's friend called and said that the special delivery just left the warehouse. He has about seven stops before he gets out of the city, so Tim says it might be okay to grab a burger or something?"

The truck stop had orders to go and tables to eat at. It was crowded. Tim and Doris grabbed a booth for two in the back of the restaurant. Jimmy and our two Russians managed seats at the counter.

"Order me a sandwich to go and a large coffee," I told Jimmy. "I'll wait outside in the Hummer."

I was about to walk across the lot to where we had parked when I noticed a black Jeep pulled off the road on the side of the four-lane highway. It was about two hundred yards behind our vehicles. Someone was following us.

I didn't think it was Colonel Kim and his torpedoes. He'd be following the FedEx truck. I had to think fast.

Who would be looking for the magician at this stage of the game? The Confederates were in jail. Marcy was long gone. Most of the other players were dead. Who would think they had anything to gain? Maybe it was someone who still believed that Zeke had pocketed the two million and knew we were on his trail?

Two guys came out of the truck stop and headed for a pickup truck next to the door.

"Excuse me," I said. "If you're headed back toward town, could I get a lift just opposite where that Jeep is? I have a sore knee, and I need to get back there. I just phoned for road service from the rental company."

"No sweat. Hop in."

I jumped out opposite the Jeep. The pickup took off. I slid down the embankment and worked my way past the Jeep on the opposite side of the road. I poked my head up for a look. They were people I knew, people who didn't accept a break when they caught one.

I sent a text to Jimmy: Blk Jeep Bhind R Cars. 3 stooges. IM across road.

Jimmy's return text read: Sta put calling sheriff on outstanding warrants.

Ten minutes brought three cop cars. Ten minutes later, Detective Jake Glover arrived with Detective Duffy at the wheel.

"This kind of cooperation keeps up; I'm gonna have to put you and Jimmy on the payroll," Glover said.

The handcuffed Cavaretta trio was tossed into the back of Glover's cruiser. He turned to one of the county cops.

"I'll take it from here. These boys like to escape, but I don't think they can outrun Duffy's double aught shotgun."

CHAPTER TWENTY-FOUR

Our caravan left metro Vegas behind. Along the main highway were hundreds of square miles of desert. We were on the alert for green mile markers and scrub vegetation. Those were the clues to finding Zeke's place.

Jimmy grumbled as he over-steered the too loud Hummer.

"You know what they should call these buggies?" he asked.

"The George W. Bush Do-it-yourself Hearse?" I asked.

"Over-priced Piece of Shit sounds about right."

"And one of your own choosing," I added.

"Think it has the Donald Rumsfeld cardboard floor shields to deflect IEDs?"

"Run over a land mine, and we'll try it out," I said.

We both had the grumbles, and they weren't just coming from the Nation Builder Special we were riding in. Big question marks were waiting for us at Zeke's place. Jacky had gotten the idea from Gene Cornell that our group could rearrange a few deck chairs with Zeke, and everything would be "Mission Accomplished." The Charlemagne Show or a facsimile of it would be back to drawing huge crowds at the Galloping Dominos.

In their desire to declare victory, and rake in dollars, they hadn't figured on the blabbermouth factor. Could clowns like the Cavaretta brothers, Fitch and Rice, Sammy Di Carlo, the Confederate Front, and Colonel Kim and his cronies keep their traps shut about the mysterious toys from Area 51?

Already things had gone off the track when Fitch and Rice produced a Doris golem. How many other golem hookers were wandering around Vegas casinos? Fitch and Rice might have created dozens.

My cell phone rang. I must have been sending waves of grumble toward Chicago. It was Dawn, being the concerned spouse.

"Where are you, Nick? Are you with Jimmy? Cassandra says you two are trying to put together a deal with the Russians to get Charlemagne back into the theater."

"Yeah, we're riding in a rented dream car of Jimmy's, on our way to see Zeke."

"Put me on speaker. I want Jimmy to hear me."

"Hey, Dawn," Jimmy yelled.

"What's all the noise?" she asked. "Sounds like you're in a factory."

"It's a Hummer," Jimmy yelled.

"A bummer? You can say that again. I can hardly hear you."

"It's a noisy Jeep," I yelled.

"Cheap? It sounds like it."

"We're on our way to the desert," Jimmy said. "Trying to straighten things out."

"You guys aren't miracle workers," Dawn said. "Jacky and Muriel can moan all they want. That doesn't do your blood pressure any favors. Jimmy, Cassandra says you're taking Losartan. Well, Nick's on Norvasc. See, blood brothers, like you've always been. Only this time, it's blood pressure brothers. We love you both. We just don't want you boys to do something rash."

"We love you, too." We both yelled.

"Yeah, like I said, you're not miracle workers. Don't do anything rash."

"We should have you come out and visit," Jimmy said. "Cassandra can get us comp tickets to some of the shows."

"I'd love it," she said. "You boys take care, I can't yell anymore."

She rang off.

"When did we ever do anything rash?" I asked.

"What does she mean, we're not miracle workers?" Jimmy asked.

We rolled along, heatwaves floated off the road, creating mirages of water shimmering ahead.

"I should have listened to Tim," Jimmy said. "He warned me about renting this Hummer. He drove one of these things in

Disappearing Act

Afghanistan when he was in the service. He was an O-1, a second Looie over there. He took a couple in his leg. Damn near bled to death. Says he still feels the pain at times."

"I know he's had shit for help from the VA," I said. "He's still looking for steady work."

Ahead, Tim slowed down in the lead vehicle. We were getting close. Soon we were at a crawl. He turned off the highway onto a desert trail marked only by a rotting fence post. About a hundred yards off the main road, we stopped and got out of the vehicles.

"It looks pretty rough," Tim said. "There are a few places up ahead that look like desert washes, where some of that heavy rain might have come through yesterday. I notice it's clouding up. We don't want to get caught in any downpour when we're stuck in one of the washes."

"Da," Boris said. "Nick never say about bringing water wings to desert party."

"Just the luck," Alexi said. "Drown in desert."

"It's about a half-mile in, as I recall," Tim said. "Might be a good time to call and tell them we're coming in."

I looked at Doris.

"Tim knows about most of why we're here." Doris blushed.

I wondered if she blushed on purpose.

"No need to call," Alexi said. "I just talk to him. I tell him two SUVs being chased into property by cowboy realtor Butch Cassidy."

The busted-up road was a roller coaster ride for the next half mile. We arrived at a low-slung ranch style home fifty yards from a large metal barn. John stood with a rifle next to Zeke on the shaded porch of the house.

We went inside and sat down in the large living room.

Cold beers got everyone cooled off.

"I know all the reasons you're here," Zeke said. "I have to tell you out in front that I can't see going back to Dominos or anywhere else and doing the show with the equipment I used. It's way too risky. Look at the creeps we've been trying to avoid. How many people are dead or in jail?"

I looked across from where Jimmy and I sat. Tim was holding hands with Doris. She no longer had the ponytails on each side of her head. Her red hair was combed out into a shag cut, and she was smiling at him. She wasn't Jimmy's daughter Rachel, but she was doing a damn good job of looking like her.

Zeke was about to say something but paused. He looked worried

"I don't mean to be out of line," Tim said, "But is there any way that you can help Doris with her problem?"

Boris and Alexi looked at each other and shrugged.

"Jimmy daughter having problem?" Alexi asked.

"I'll tell you what happened," Jimmy said. "Those two assholes Fitch and Rice made a golem that looks like Doris and turned it into a prostitute at New York, New York."

"No," Alexi said. "I kill them if not already dead."

"I think I can help," Zeke said. "I don't have the toys Fitch and Rice used, but…"

"I have them," I said. "Hope that makes things better."

I slid the "Welcome to Las Vegas" bag toward Zeke. He looked inside.

"This wouldn't be what they were calling 'The Magic Carpet,' would it?"

I was about to answer when we heard a truck pull up outside. The FedEx delivery had arrived.

John went to the door.

"Package for Ted Evans."

"I'll sign it," John said. "This your last stop?"

"Yeah, the guys delivering your all-terrain vehicles, the ATVs are unloading them off a truck just off the highway."

"That right?"

"Ran into them having coffee up the road. They asked if I knew where your place was. Turned out we were both headed here."

I reached for the FedEx envelope and started to open it. Tucked into the sealing tape was a small sensor. Colonel Kim and his crew had a tracking device on it.

The FedEx truck bounced its way back toward the highway.

Tim stood next to me, watching it leave.

"Nick, as I understand the situation, we may soon be under attack. As far as arms go, John's got this old Remington. I know you've got a Glock. Doris has a Ruger."

"And Jimmy's got his golf bag," Jimmy said, dragging it from the Hummer to the house. "It's a Springfield with a scope and a couple hundred rounds."

"He stole it from Ernest Hemingway," I said.

"And Boris has AK-47," Boris said. "Proudly stolen from Putin. Why steal from famous writer when you can steal from greedy dictator?"

I showed Tim the envelope with the sensor attached. He thought a moment.

"From what I gather, what's his name, Colonel Kim?"

I nodded.

"Maybe the colonel has a force of four, five?"

"Could be," I said.

"They didn't follow us out here," Tim said. "They followed FedEx, so they don't know that our group is here. We've got that advantage on them. The tracking device seems to indicate they'll try a nighttime assault. Probably think that Zeke is here alone or maybe with John. They'll work their way in slowly using the tracker and come in expecting little or no resistance."

"What about the rain?" I asked. "Won't that screw things up for them?"

"Maybe for a bit, but if they're determined and equipped right, they'll stay on the attack. They see little resistance and high reward on their end."

Jimmy found his binoculars in the golf bag. We grabbed an extension ladder and propped it on the side of the barn and went up to take a look.

"Sons-a-bitches have a couple ATVs just sitting there next to a flatbed truck," Jimmy said. "Looks like the two torpedoes, Colonel Kim and someone wearing fatigues and a Desert Storm helmet."

Tim took the binoculars.

"Someone black, carrying an assault rifle," He said. "Damn, could be a woman."

"Pipes?" Jimmy and I both asked.

"Pipe hitter," Tim said. "A pro, maybe."

Back on the ground, I asked Boris about Pipes.

"Da. Back in Africa, she was pipefitter for defense force. I tell Kim if Pipes sing good, we can work visa for plumber. Congressman in Chicago like donation."

"Not pipefitter," Tim said. "Pipe hitter. Military slang for a special forces sharpshooter."

CHAPTER TWENTY-FIVE

Jimmy and Tim were atop the metal barn, keeping an eye on the main highway where Colonel Kim and company were prepping their ATVs for an assault on Zeke's place.

"They've moved their vehicles down the road a half-mile," Tim yelled. "Terrain looks better there for the ATVs."

Boris and Alexi moved our vehicles into the large metal barn, out of sight of our invaders.

"Valet parking job in desert," Boris said. "Nick and Jimmy lousy tippers."

"Yeah, go broke and die thirsty," Alexi said. "Good, we bring beer in ice chest."

I walked back into the house. In the kitchen, Zeke sat with Doris. The Area 51 toys were spread out on the table.

"I couldn't help Doris with the toys I had, so I'm going to try the Magic Carpet toys," Zeke said.

I had wondered about the toys and their powers but watching them work was close to questioning your sanity. I was about to enter a special effects movie, only everything would really be happening.

Zeke pressed some buttons on what looked like an iPhone, and one of the pieces on the table floated up and started to grow. It became a transparent screen with images on it. It was about three feet square and paper-thin. The visuals were geometric shapes of blue and red.

"At this stage, you can walk right through the display," Zeke said. He put his hand through it and waved. The shapes in the display stayed where they were.

He pressed another button and grabbed an edge of the floating display. Now it was rubbery and about an inch thick. He stretched it and let go. It bounced back into shape, still floating above the table.

After pressing more buttons, the display was solid and opaque.

"Feel it," he said. "It's like carbon steel."

It felt cold and heavy. It was six inches thick. I tried to move it. It wouldn't budge. It continued floating above the table. On its flat surface were images of Doris, kneeling naked on a blue pad.

"This is the last file executed on the Magic Carpet," Zeke said. "The toys I worked with were similar, but never had this much power. I'm not plugged into any power source. I suspect we're getting a flow from a source we can't see. It's that other reality theory we talked about, connected to another dimension."

"Wow, that's me," Doris said. "This is embarrassing. My thighs are too fat, and my butt looks funny."

"It's the electronic lens configuration," Zeke said. "There are no glass lenses. It's all momentary molecular configurations. Just like the display itself. One time it's a cloud, another time, funny rubber, and again solid steel."

"Can you help me?" Doris asked.

"Luckily, yes," Zeke said. "Yours being the last file lets us erase whatever was created. Your golem is about to disappear. When I was creating the Charlemagne golem, I came up with several bad ones. I'd hit the cancel switch, and they'd disappear. Sometimes it would take several hours to disappear them, depending on how much work had gone into creating them."

Zeke's finger hit two buttons, and the Doris display disappeared. In its place was a screen full of hundreds of geometric shapes. One in the middle of the pattern was flashing green.

"That's the device asking us to match up a shape that will let us into the next file. On the toys I used, there were only 9 tiles to match with. If you chose wrong, the device flashed another shape, and you'd have to start all over again. It creates a different code sequence each time. I suspect that my device was a controller for the magic carpet. Maybe the difference between a laptop and a mainframe computer."

"Is my golem gone?" Doris asked.

"If not now, soon," Zeke said. "Certainly in a few hours."

"I can't tell you how happy that makes me," she said. "I want to make a new start. I've lost my fascination for dysfunctional assholes."

Zeke smiled and pressed a few more buttons, and the display collapsed into a small rectangle similar to an iPad. He put all the toys into the Vegas shopping bag.

"I know how she feels, I don't want to screw around with this stuff anymore," he said. "When I was doing the Charlemagne show, spurious signals would affect neon signs along the Strip. TV broadcasts were compromised. Once, I heard that a brief portion of our show flashed across a news broadcast for about four seconds. It made me wonder what else was I troubling – the genetics of those watching the show? I started to feel like one of those clowns who push nuclear reactors or fracking with wastewater."

"You should feel better," Doris said. "You've done a wonderful favor for me, getting rid of my hooker golem and making me realize how out of step I've been."

"It wasn't just you," Zeke said. "I got a case of arrogance playing with the toys. The Ezekiel coins are small golems that I created out of thin air, just like you saw me punch up the display screen out of nowhere. I acted like some petty god."

He went over to the closet and returned with his baseball bat.

"This is another attempt at arrogance," he said. "I couldn't leave the game alone. I had to invent something to tamper with it, screw things up."

I had heard about the bat from Karen, the manager of the Vegas Dykes. It could put funny spins on a batted ball that could drive a fielder crazy. The bat was light-weight and had a knob that could be turned for various settings. It felt good, yet something about it was alien. I handed it back to Zeke. He dropped it into the bag of toys.

I could identify with both Doris and Zeke. If you were lucky, there came time to put away all the acts that got in your way. For me, it was the tough guy act, the guy with the hair-trigger temper that created maybe more problems than he solved.

A seed of doubt was growing in my mind. Somewhere had I missed something? Would it all come down to a shoot-out with the Colonel Kim quartet? What about the Area 51 toys? They were as dangerous as Hell. What do you do with them, even if you drive off the evil forces? The government didn't even acknowledge them.

I grabbed a beer out of the fridge and sat down in the living room. What had I missed? Was it something I had seen, but it hadn't registered?

I thought about the Cavaretta brothers in the black Jeep. I remembered several black Jeeps following us down the highway. One had a yellow antenna ball, the other had a blue one. Another might have been red. I figured. Jeeps were the standard ride for people heading to the desert. Vegas rented them by the dozens. The yellow ball belonged to the Cavarettas. What happened to the Jeep with the blue antenna ball, or the red one? It hadn't passed us when we entered the truck stop. Traffic was thin by then. I didn't recall anyone passing us. No black Jeep showed up, except the one the Cavarettas sat in.

Second thoughts were giving way to third and fourth thoughts. I was over-thinking. As dusk came, we had to be alert for Colonel Kim's attack. I could say to Hell with the second black Jeep.

Or could I?

My cell phone rang.

It was Roland.

"Nick, you heard the news?"

"No, what?"

"Glover and Duffy got shot. The Cavarettas are in the wind, my friend. Cops figure they had an accomplice. Happened about a mile down from the truck stop out on the highway. Both are unconscious—Fifty-fifty on the prognosis.

"Any witnesses?"

"A couple iffys. Someone saw a black panel truck. Another guy says it was a Jeep with a blue antenna ball. They asked the guy the color of the Jeep, and he couldn't remember."

My eyes fell to the FedEx envelope on the coffee table. I picked it up to look at it again. But wait. There was another FedEx envelope stuck to the back of the one I had in my hands. A small sensor hung from the sealing tape, announcing to whoever was tracking us that we were where we were, ready for the pickings. The delivery ticket told precisely where we were, addressed to Mr.

Ted Evans. I looked at the space for the sender, and a big part of it came into focus.

"Roland, could you check on one more thing?"

He took down the info and said he'd get right back.

It was one of the oldest tricks in the book, and I had fallen for it. Lure some people into thinking you're going to do something and let them run with their logic. It was how draw plays and screen plays worked in football and changeups in baseball. You needed a hungry sucker anxious to get things settled. Let them jump to their conclusions. I was that sucker. I had jumped.

I heard Jimmy yelling from the roof of the metal barn.

I went to the front screen door of Zeke's house. The sky was dark. It was late afternoon. A large thunderhead was moving in. Light rain fell.

"The FedEx truck is coming back," Jimmy said. "Kim's group is coming, too, from down the highway off to our right."

Jimmy and Tim scrambled off the roof and into the side door of the metal barn.

Boris and Alexi swung the large doors to the barn closed, hiding our vehicles.

John came into the house and grabbed the Remington. He knelt next to the living room window.

"I ain't taking any terrorist shit," he said. "It's time we met them with lead."

Doris moved to the floor next to him, behind the couch. Zeke stood and walked toward the front door where I stood.

"Why's FedEx coming back?" Zeke asked.

My cell phone rang.

"Your guess was right," Roland said. "She never got on that flight to Caracas."

I looked at the FedEx envelope again. The sender was Marcy Feldstein.

"She just stepped out of a FedEx truck holding an assault rifle," I said. "The Cavaretta brothers are with her."

CHAPTER TWENTY-SIX

Marcy Feldstein stood next to the FedEx truck. She had an AR-15 in her hand. Vito Cavaretta stood beside her with what looked like a Smith & Wesson 38. Pete Cavaretta shoved the duct-taped FedEx driver out the truck side door. He stumbled and fell into the sand next to the driveway. The rain started with big drops the size of Ezekiel coins.

I figured we'd have no trouble taking down Marcy and the Cavarettas. We had the Springfield and the AK 47 in the metal barn. In the house, John was ready with his Remington, and I was prepared to reach for my Glock. The last thing we expected was Zeke trying for the Nobel Peace Prize.

He opened the front screen door and stepped onto the covered porch, raising his hands.

"Been a while, Marcy. Thought you took off for Caracas."

"I like to keep people guessing," she said. "You know what I'm here for."

"You grabbed the two million dollars that Jerry and Neal held back. For a while, Jacky thought I ran off with it. That could have gotten me killed."

"You play the game with the big boys, you take your chances, Zeke."

"Now you want the toys. You must have big ideas. The toys are dangerous."

"Yeah, like my friends in Caracas give a fuck about that. I've already shot two cops today. I'm dangerous, too. I don't mind icing you or anyone else who gets in the way."

Zeke stood in silence. His peacekeeping mission was falling on deaf ears.

Disappearing Act

I could hear the hum of small engines off to the side of the house. I figured it was the Colonel Kim party of four.

I went toward the back door, too late. Pipes busted in, pointing her assault rifle at me.

"I want the toys, or you'll die," she said.

"I almost liked you better as a singer," I said.

"Put your gun on the floor and kick it toward me."

I did as she asked.

"Are you with the Avon lady outside?" I asked. "I believe she's already made arrangements to purchase the toys."

"Yeah, like uh Hell." It was Colonel Kim, still dressed in his tinhorn dictator's outfit--shades, blazer, silk ascot. He leaned down to brush the sand off his pants and loafers.

"You better talk to our manager," I said. "He's out on the porch talking with Mrs. Feldstein about big money. Two million bucks. You got that much?"

I noticed John and Doris huddled next to the couch by the window.

John nodded. He had the Remington ready. They were out of sight of Pipes and Kim.

I looked out the side window. Next to the metal barn side door, one of Kim's torpedoes was making his way to take a shot at Marcy and the Cavarettas.

The rain came slowly in big drops. Thunder and lightning in the distance were coming toward us, pushed by a wind that gathered speed.

"Can't we talk, Marcy?" Zeke asked from the front porch.

"I'm done fucking with you, Zeke."

She fired a single shot into the dirt in front of Zeke.

Lightning struck nearby with a thunderous crash.

Colonel Kim's torpedo by the metal barn was about to step into the open and fire. Tim stepped out of the door behind him and garroted him with a length of wire. Jimmy grabbed his weapon. They dragged their victim into the barn.

Torpedo Number Two crept up the driver's side of the FedEx truck. Big mistake. Ralphie Cavaretta shoved his revolver out the window to the torpedo's head and fired three times. He fell next to where the FedEx driver sat duct-taped.

Lightning struck the metal roof of the barn with a loud bang. Zeke jumped back into the house through the living room door. The sky was a dark grey. Lightning struck again, this time bouncing off the roof and landing on the FedEx truck.

I looked back at where Pipes and Colonel Kim stood next to the kitchen table. Something strange was happening in the Welcome to Vegas bag. A blue glow was coming from it. A high-pitched hum like a smoke alarm filled the house.

Colonel Kim grabbed the bag and started for the back door. He opened it to Ralphie Cavaretta standing with his 38.

"Not so fast, Gook."

Ralphie grabbed for the bag and fired twice into Kim's chest. Kim dropped to the floor with the bag. It was glowing red now.

Pipes turned and riddled Ralphie with a long burst from her rifle. She grabbed for the glowing bag on the floor.

John stepped into the room and fired.

Pipes crumpled to the floor backward. Blood gushed from a bullet hole in her chest.

Doris screamed.

Pipes looked up at John and tried to raise her rifle to shoot.

John chambered another round into the Remington and shot Pipes between the eyes.

"Not in this reality, Sister," John said.

The red glow was intense, coming from the bag. It looked like the house would catch fire.

Lightning struck again.

Marcy and the two Cavarettas charged toward the front door. The barn doors swung open. The Springfield and the AK 47 barked hot lead. Vito fell first, in front of the FedEx truck. Pete turned to return fire at the barn doors and caught the full barrage. He fell facedown into a puddle.

As Marcy burst through the front door, the firing from the metal barn stopped. She pointed the AR-15 at Zeke and then me.

"I knew you'd be involved in this, Nick," she said. "The Cavarettas gave me a full line-up of who to expect."

"What's your next move, Marcy? Looks like all your boys are dead. So's the competition."

I motioned over to where Colonel Kim, Pipes, and Ralphie sprawled in pools of blood.

"Just as well, Nick. It's only me, the toys and the money."

She kicked my Glock toward the front door and motioned toward John.

"Rifle on the floor, Gramps. Zeke and Nick get over there with the old-timer and the girl."

She walked over to where Kim fell and took a large envelope out of his jacket.

"Six million in bearer bonds," she said. "Another dumb son of a bitch."

She looked at Doris.

"Let's go, Sugar. We're getting in that FedEx truck out there. I'm using you as my passage out of here. Nick, tell your boys in that barn that I'm coming out with what's-her-name here. I've got a full load, so don't fuck with me."

She grabbed John's Remington and tossed it out the front door. My Glock was next, landing in a puddle next to Pete Cavaretta's body.

"Tell them, Nick," she said.

I went to the door.

"Hey, guys, Marcy's coming out. She's got Doris for a hostage. Hold your fire. She's got a full load in the AR-15. Let her go."

They stepped out onto the porch and took the step down onto the wet graveled driveway, working their way past Pete's body. Marcy held the glowing bag in her left hand and the AR-15 in her right.

They were stepping around Vito's corpse when Doris turned and pulled her Ruger out of her jacket and aimed it at Marcy's face. Marcy stepped back. The Ruger clicked on the empty chamber.

Marcy started to laugh as she raised the AR-15.

"Dumb bitch."

Doris pulled the trigger again. The loud blank went off in Marcy's face. She stepped back, bewildered that she wasn't hit. Then she charged Doris. The third shot was waiting for her. The real load blew pieces of Marcy's head toward the puddle that held Pete Cavaretta.

Doris dropped the Ruger and sank to her knees in the wet gravel. She tried to catch her breath and scream at the same time. Her tears flowed as she shook.

Tim rushed out of the metal barn and dropped to his knees, hugging her.

"Way too much, Tim," she said. "I've had way too much from bitches who think they own you."

Zeke came out of the house and grabbed the glowing bag that held the toys, the bat, and the Ezekiel coins.

"This has to end," he said. "This is madness."

In the distance, the sound of a helicopter approached. A glowing light pointed at us. It was the same glow that was coming from the bag Zeke held. He ran down the driveway toward the craft as it got lower.

Jimmy looked at me and shrugged.

"Cops? Feds?"

"Let him go," I said. "He's trying to square the books."

Jimmy stared at the hovering craft.

"Not cops," he said. "Definitely not cops."

It wasn't a helicopter. It was huge, like the craft the original Ezekiel had described.

A wheel turned within a wheel, and a whirlwind came out of it in a great cloud, with a fire folding on itself, and out of the middle was the color of amber, out of the midst of the fire. Lights flashed along the craft's length, and the smoke alarm whine became a low-frequency hum that changed pitch in a one-two-three pattern.

Zeke ran through the rain down the road to where the craft hovered. Lightning flashed. The torrential rain fell. The ship glowed red and then blue. An object floated toward the ship on a golden beam. It was the Welcome to Las Vegas bag, now glowing a peaceful blue as it entered.

"Dasvidanya," Boris said.

"Na Zdorovie," Alexi said, raising his can of beer.

The lights on the craft flashed green and went out.

The rain stopped.

We stared up at a clear desert sky full of stars.

The craft was gone.

CHAPTER TWENTY-SEVEN

My tale didn't end with toys levitating into the Ezekiel craft as our group cheered.

Reality has a habit of intruding on Spielberg endings.

There were loose ends.

For starters, there were eight dead bodies and a duct-taped FedEx driver to deal with.

Tim McKnight, the ex-GI and Doris Day, the ex-hooker, had had a memorable first date. Tim had strangled a hired killer, and Doris had shot Marcy Feldstein in the face. What a story to tell your kids.

Then there was Zeke, who had produced magic and now had no toys to work with. Zeke's buddy John had gone from a charming old gent who told stories to someone who could pump two slugs into a sniper when the chips were down.

I thought about how strange it was. Since my arrival in Vegas, there were fifteen dead, three in jail, and two in intensive care with gunshot wounds. I hadn't fired a shot during that time. I could have left the Glock at home.

Boris was at least up for rearranging the deck chairs.

"Is big wood table in back of barn, plenty old chairs, next to beer-cooler. We bring our people in there, away from dead bodies while we figure out."

We got Danny, the FedEx guy un-duct-taped, and sat him down in the barn with Doris and Tim. John brought some whiskey from the house to drink with them.

Disappearing Act

Zeke sat on the front porch of the house. He kept repeating, "This was a religious experience. We've delivered the toys. We've delivered ourselves."

He stared at the clear night sky.

The desert was cooling down. The smell of the gun battle hung in the air.

I got the envelope from Marcy's body – the one she took from Colonel Kim's body. The bearer bonds were there, six million bucks worth. Her valise was inside the FedEx truck. Inside it was cashier's checks totaling two million bucks, just the way Jacky liked to get paid.

We had found his money, lost his magic show forever, and gotten six million vig on the side. Somehow, I had to become Solomon. Figuring out the split at Ribs by Gus seemed like a walk in the park compared to this.

"We can play this as a home invasion by desperate killers," Jimmy said. "Who the Hell would believe magical toys. Maybe that FedEx guy didn't hear or see much. I don't think he saw the hovercraft, or whatever it was."

"He needs more beer in his system," I said. "See if you can get Tim to help with that. Boris is good for that, too. Tell him the cops are on their way. Everyone needs to stay cool."

The cops were on their way, according to Roland. He called my cell phone from a Metro helicopter.

"Nick, we're on a patch-through. That means that we're open to listeners who can hear where you buried the family jewels," he laughed and said, "Over."

"Good to hear from you," I said. "Things are under control. We had a home invasion, but we've managed to defend ourselves. All eight intruders are dead. Over."

"Would some be the four fugitives from the shootings of the two detectives? Over."

"Yes, and one would be from the South Korean mafia, Jo-Pok. Another is an undocumented Congo sniper. Two others might be local thugs. All DOA. Over."

"Any injuries to your people? Over."

"A FedEx driver got roughed-up. Maybe a bit confused. It could need some attention. Over"

"We're ten minutes out from you, with ground help on the way about 20 minutes out. Over."

"Can you do a large sweep with lights over our area to see if there's anyone else out there in the desert? Over."

"Will do. See you soon. Out."

Boris made sure that Danny, the FedEx driver, was watching as the helicopter made its sweeps above us.

"Is back again," Boris said. "This time, no rain, yeah. We celebrate, have shot and beer."

I walked over to Zeke and told him the cops were about to land. We needed to get our stories straight.

"Tell me," he said.

"We all came out here to discuss a possible new show at the Galloping Dominos. You produced the former show there with help from John. Jimmy and I represent the new owner of the casino. Boris and Alexi represent Gene Cornell, who represents the hottest singer on North America Loves Music. Doris and Tim are personal assistants of mine. Got it?"

"So why did Marcy and company come here?" Zeke asked.

"They needed a hideout. She'd been out here on a visit six months ago with her husband after one of your shows. She didn't think you were in town."

"That should work," he said. "Tell the others."

We did.

Roland landed with two cops and an assistant chief.

I told the story as our group gathered around.

Assistant Chief Miller looked at the large puddle holding the bodies of Marcy Feldstein and Pete Cavaretta.

"These are the pieces of shit that tried to kill Glover and Duffy?"

"They are," Roland said. "These folks may be getting a reward."

"I like it when citizens fight back," Miller said. "Show me more bodies."

It was after eleven when we pulled up outside Rusty's. Jimmy and I walked to the back booth, where Cassandra sat licking salt from her margarita glass.

"Jesus," she said. "Eight dead. You two really did it this time. I hear you're going to share in a reward with the rest of your crew. Fifty thousand dollars. Word is that Glover and Duffy will pull through. Where's the rest of your group?"

"I put everybody up at Bellagio for the night, on Jacky," I said. "We've got his two million back. That ought to make him happy."

We shared some food and drinks, and it was time to leave. We'd attack the loose ends in the morning, or so I thought.

The message at Bellagio was, "Call Jacky Immediately."

"Nick, here's what Gene and I decided on the theater," he began. "He can get the whole North America Loves Music show produced from our theater. There will be try-outs, big television productions and a lot of people coming to support entertainers. It's a constant flow of money. Tee shirts, hats, you name it. We need that Zeke guy to be in charge of the production end. He's got his assistants, no?"

He rattled on like that for another twenty minutes. The Galloping Dominos was his new toy. He'd have high culture by building a museum that would display Middle East artifacts on loan from museums in Chicago, New York, and Israel. Muriel and Dawn would cover that. There would also be a skateboard racetrack stadium that would seat three thousand. Skateboarders would run head-to-head over the intricate course for large purses. The competitions would be available for a fee on cable and the Internet.

He finally ran out of gas, or so I thought.

I told him about the eight dead and how the toys were back on the Ezekiel craft with their rightful owners.

"Jesus, the Ezekiel craft," he said. "What are they? Aliens? Part of that Area 51 stuff the government runs?"

"Don't know," I said. "Definitely out of our league."

"Yeah, better leave that one alone."

I told him Jimmy, and I had recovered his two million bucks.

"Good, good," he said. "I didn't think I'd see any of it. You've had a Hell of a time. Listen, send me a million of it. No, better yet give it to the accountants when they show up tomorrow. You split the other million up with Jimmy and whoever helped you."

"What's the catch, Jacky?"

"I'm thinking you might want to put some of it into a house out there. I'm going to need you and Dawn to oversee part of the operation out there, Jimmy and Cassandra, too. You know, Nick, people I can trust."

"And what would you say if I told you I had found six million bucks and was ready to walk away?" I asked.

"I'd tell you to put all six million on red and cross your fingers. You're tired. Go to bed, Nick. We got a lot of work ahead of us."

In eight months, the Dominos had a new face and a new feel to it. The theatre and the skateboard track were both busy. The main lobby had a permanent display of trophies and pictures of our sponsored softball team, the Vegas Dykes.

The Middle East Museum was about to open with Dawn in charge.

"This is one of my dreams," the World's Sexiest Blonde said to her handsome husband. "I want people to understand that we're all one people with so many common traditions. Imagine, it took a couple tough guys like you and Jimmy to make it happen."

I loved it when she called us tough guys.

Stories still made the rounds about johns who had been in mid-act with assorted hookers only to have them suddenly disappear. Apparently, those aboard the Ezekiel craft had erased every golem created by the toys. How many golem hookers had suddenly booked was anyone's guess.

Zeke had his million to do with what he wanted. He had trained Tim in all phases of running the theatre and now was taking John for an extended world tour.

"Jesus, he's eighty-eight," Zeke said. "Could be his last chance to see it all."

"Keep the beer cold," John said. "I'll have some good stories when we get back."

Tim married the hostess of North America Loves Music and changed her name from Doris Day to Doris McKnight. Jimmy was proud to walk the bride up the aisle and give her away. Part of the McKnights' million-dollar share bought an apartment at City Center.

Boris and Alexi each got their million and regularly brought in new performers to try out for North America Loves Music.

"We start fund, so Gene's kids don't starve, go to Northwestern instead," Alexi said.

"Da, this show biz stuff shaky," Boris said. "But benefits good." He patted the ass of the curvy brunette he had brought for an audition.

Jimmy supervised the Galloping Dominos in-house legal staff. His chief attorney was homerun-hitting Marlene Baker of the Vegas Dykes.

With his new wealth, Jimmy decided there was something he and Cassandra needed to have, Neal Braxton's old home.

"It's got everything we've always wanted," he said. "There's a crime scene story right outside the front door. There might be money hidden in the place, and there are great neighbors across the fairway."

He was right. We had the same thing. We hadn't had a shooting outside the front door, but there had been one nearby. We didn't think there was money hidden in our house, but we did have Jimmy and Cassandra's house across the fairway.

We had our own treasure. We had three-year-old Molly, who drew pictures of Seymour the Sun Bear. Seymour looked just like the pictures she drew of her dad.

The End.

ABOUT THE AUTHOR

Ray Pace writes stories about the Hemingway brothers, black bear detectives who investigate fairy tales, ghost tours, and the crazy world of Las Vegas wise guys. He lives in Waikoloa Village on the Big Island of Hawaii. You can find his books on Amazon.com.

https://amzn.to/3rveQzH